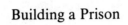

Building a Prison

VLADIMIR KORNILOV

Building a Prison

Translated by Edward Dale

5077

Quartet Books
London Melbourne New York

Published by Quartet Books Limited 1984
A member of the Namara Group
27/29 Goodge Street, London W1P 1FD

Translated from the Russian *Kamenshchik, Kamenshchik*

British Library Cataloguing in Publication Data

Kornilov, Vladimir
    Building a prison.
    I. Title
    891.73′44[F]   PG3482.7.R591/

ISBN 0-7043-2441-5

Photoset by AKM Associates (UK) Ltd, Southall, Greater London
Printed and bound in Great Britain by
Mackays of Chatham Ltd, Kent

Translator's Note

Russians are normally addressed formally by their name and patronymic, and informally by diminutives (of which there are a great many) formed from their first names. To reduce possible confusion, the use of these forms has been kept to a minimum in the translation. For the reader's convenience a list of the main characters is given at the beginning of the book.

Principal Characters in
Building a Prison

Pavel Rodionovich CHOLYSHEV (Pashka, Pasha, Pashet): born 1902

Yevgenia Sergeyevna CHOLYSHEV (Zhenya, Zheka): his second wife, born 1920

Lyubov Simonovna (Lyuba): Cholyshev's mother

Klim Kornienko: Cholyshev's uncle (Lyubov's brother), a priest

Leokadia: Klim's wife

Varvara Alekseyevna (Bronka): Cholyshev's first wife

Maria Pavlovna (Masha): Cholyshev's daughter, born 1929

Grigory Yakovlevich TOKAREV (also TOKAR) (Grisha, Grishka): later Masha's husband, born about 1927

Svetlana: daughter of Masha and Grisha

Nadya (Nadka): Grisha's sister

Dora Isaakovna TOKAR: Grisha's and Nadya's mother

Yudif: Dora's sister

Doctor TOKAR (Aron Solomonovich)

Rosa (Rosalia Arkadievna): Dr Tokar's wife

Mikhail Stepanich: in Civil War a Red (Bolshevik) partisan, during World War II the head of a Workers' Supplies Board in Siberia

Susanna Fyodorovna: a Moscow friend of Dora Tokar

A Communist Party functionary from Moscow

Filipp Semyonovich: a hospital patient

Building a Prison

At the age of seventy-one, Pavel Cholyshev was pitifully boyish-looking. Small and gaunt, with a little crest of grey hair popping up on top of his head, he even took offence in an un-grown-up way.

'Pashet, you don't know how to lose your temper, so don't bother trying!' the old man's second wife, Zhenya, would laugh. She was much younger than Pavel, and he adored her, but had convinced himself that she would leave him. Sooner or later she would dance off to some successful colleague of hers and stay with him for ever. Zhenya was full of charm, Zhenya was clever. Whereas he, Cholyshev, always had been a mediocrity, and now – a pensioner for longer than he cared to remember – he was a complete zero.

Every morning, the door would scarcely have banged shut behind his wife when the old man would feel suffocated with fear of being abandoned. By evening this foreboding would turn into certainty: it was all over, his wife would not return, there was nothing to live for . . .

An hour would pass. Then another. Then a third. The old man, like a punished child, would wallow in his sense of being deserted, or gravely ill, or even dead, and Zhenya would then have to spend a long time pulling him back from this pale of dejection.

'What's the matter with you? I was held up, that's all . . . I'm a typically harassed Soviet woman – and a Muscovite at that. In the mornings I don't like going to work, and in the evenings I can't get away.'

'It's not funny,' Cholyshev would scowl, but by morning he would calm down.

Today was Saturday. Zhenya was at home, but none the less the old man expected to be let down. And sure enough, after breakfast his wife opened her bureau to reveal a typewriter and some bulging, untidy-looking notebooks, and shut him up with the words: 'Don't disturb me until two.'

She's going to be typing out Grishka's work, Cholyshev guessed.

Grishka, or Grigory Yakovlevich Tokarev, his son-in-law, was a writer, or rather, a critic.

But Zhenya was not content with just the typewriter and notebooks. She carefully placed a pile of books in soft and hard covers on top of the bureau, as though decorating the room.

What does she need them for? The old man frowned, and shuffled into the kitchen in search of some housework to keep himself busy. But everything was sparkling, from the sink to the white shelves. Zhenya saw to the household chores instantaneously.

'Pashet, occupy yourself with something and stop playing the martyr,' said his wife.

Cholyshev was about to pretend he had not heard, but unable to bear the solitude, he came back into the room and asked: 'Couldn't your Tokarev find a typist?'

'This can't be given to strangers,' said Zhenya with a smile, and despite her greying hair and smoke-coloured glasses, she appeared to Cholyshev exactly as on the day they had met at the end of the war. Offended that his wife's smile was directed not at him but at his son-in-law, he flourished his hand in distress, and the pile of books flew on to the floor.

'Sit down and keep out of my way. Look, you've crumpled that.' Beating her husband to it, Zhenya picked up the books. 'I've collected them for Nadya.'

Nadya, Grisha's sister and Zhenya's friend, lived in New York.

'But it's just rubbish, fit for the waste-paper bin!' said the old man.

'You and I may think so,' Zhenya agreed reluctantly, 'but it's nice for Nadya to be able to read "G. Tokarev" on the cover.'

'Why doesn't he give her that pleasure himself, then?'

'Pashet, give over. You know very well that for thirty years he's been hiding where his sister is. He's got enough problems without her: all his articles are turned down. If he started writing to America they'd immediately suspect he'd decided to defect . . .'

She should look after herself, thought Cholyshev. What's Grishka got to be saved for? He's a free agent. Whereas you depend on your job at the lab. If you're thrown out of there because of Nadya you'll never get another job: not with a blot like that on your copybook, and you're not so young, either . . .

'Tokarev's got no right exploiting you,' he said aloud.

'Exploitation! I offered to do it myself.'

'That was a mistake. You never get a break. You should watch your heart.'

'I'm just typing as I always have. And my heart's perfectly all right.'

Zhenya was expecting her husband to remind her of her angina, and she was ready to retort that she had to work anyway until she was of pension age. But he said nothing, and Zhenya gave him a conciliatory smile. 'I'm in perfect health, Pashet. And anyway, these are good memoirs. You should read them too. He mentions you, by the way, and Varvara Alekseyevna . . .'

Varvara Alekseyevna, Cholyshev's first wife, was now dying of cancer.

'He could at least leave his mother-in-law in peace,' said the old man angrily, and started walking about the room in an effort to distract his wife from her typing.

'Pashet, I did ask you to find something to do,' Zhenya burst out.

'I've got something to do. I'm watching you propagating gossip and scandal.'

Zhenya's fingers froze on the keys and her eyes blinked behind the smoky lenses. 'Before you start throwing insults around you could read it . . .'

'I've read your Grishka. And found nothing but highfalutin nonsense.'

'But this is quite different. It's memoirs, not criticism. And very talented ones, at that.'

'You'd think you had written them yourself. What are you, Siamese twins?'

'You should be ashamed, Pashet. He's your daughter's husband.'

'And your lover!' The old man flared up, and gave himself a scare.

'Oh, this is unbearable. You know perfectly well there was never anything between Tokarev and me. Poor Pashet . . . You should have married a real woman, who would have devoted her whole life to you. And I can't change now.'

'And you love Grishka!'

'Steady, now. I only praised his manuscript. Why are you tormenting me? You don't need me that much, you know.'

Cholyshev turned cold, thinking his wife was alluding to his old age and impotence.

'You don't need *all* of me. So leave me to my own devices a little.'

Now I've got a headache, she complained to herself. He's spoilt my working mood. The poor, queer old fish . . . He goes mad when I'm out somewhere, and when I'm at home he won't give me peace, either. I feel like getting straight up and going out again. What harm are Tokarev's memoirs doing him? It was so nice to get away from all the office gossip and immerse myself in the cursed past . . .

It occurred to Zhenya that she herself was a 'queer fish'.

Certainly not quite normal, she thought, giving her head a shake, as though in front of a mirror, and a greying lock of hair fell girlishly on to her cheek . . . Why have I become so attached to things that are long past? It's thirty years since I came out of camp, and I still can't forget it. Or am I afraid to forget? Why do I cling so to labour-camp memoirs, as if real life existed only there? Or is it because things haven't worked out with Pashet and me, and I'm escaping to that world where he didn't exist? The grumpy old squabbler's become quite impossible. The things he accuses me of! Suspiciousness must grow with age . . . But maybe it's not Pashet I'm running away from, but approaching old age. And I like reading about the camps and arrests because they were my youth. It's all very simple: I'm just a coward! It's not true! (She almost cried aloud.) I'm not a coward, or a masochist. Of course, my life didn't work out. But whose did, in our chaotic times . . .?

Zhenya would have gone on arguing with herself, but just then her husband grew tired of trying to guess why she was no longer typing. He hobbled to the door, and mumbled: 'I'm going to see how Varvara Alekseyevna is.'

Ever since Varvara had been discharged from hospital, riddled with cancer, the old man had visited her regularly at their daughter's flat where she lay, taking her money, oxygen bags, painkillers procured by Zhenya, and strained soups and gruels made by Zhenya. At this moment, however, he was suffering not because his first wife was fading, but his second was typing his son-in-law's manuscript.

'But I thought you weren't going today. I'm at home today,' said Zhenya.

'*That's* where you are,' said Cholyshev, nodding his head at the dog-eared notebooks, and hurried out to the lift.

'Pashet, my dear, do you think I'm doing it on purpose?'

Zhenya ran out to the landing and pulled the wilful old man back inside.

'I don't want to be apart from you,' she said. 'I'd gladly involve you in this, but you yourself don't want to. Why don't you read it? What have you got to lose? Tokarev doesn't write about the camps, but about *those* years. I can't help it, they're very close to me. At least have a look at them – I want to know what you think of them.'

In his confusion, Cholyshev allowed himself to be led over to the day-bed, obediently took a sheaf of papers from his wife, put on his glasses, and was himself amazed at his rash capitulation.

An Attempt at Biography

Behind our fence a pretty little girl was crying. I was eight years old. I lived in a detached house. I had a blue bicycle, the only Japanese one in the whole town. I was friendly with the garrison commander, Uncle August. But I was an unhappy lad. I did not even have my father's surname, which was a good communist-sounding name and almost Russian, but my mother's common Ukrainian-Jewish name – Tokar.

. . . Masha Cholyshev was standing behind our open-work fence, and her sullen father was pulling her by the hand. I felt like saying to her: 'Masha, take my bicycle – for keeps.'

There was a lot I felt like saying to her, but there was her father, who despised me. (Even now he cannot stand me, although my father has disappeared even from the small print in the *Historical Encyclopaedia*. But I am fond of Pashet Cholyshev.)

Ours was a strange family. My mother, Dora Isaakovna Tokar, was born six years before my father, and joined the Party before him, but she had a humble job, as a local education inspector. She scorned her husband's American car, lunched in the teachers' canteen, and was forever threatening to move in with her hunchbacked sister, Yudif, a dressmaker.

'Move in with devil, for all I care!' my father would shout. 'But you're not getting the children!' (That is, Nadya and me.)

Eventually their relations were severed. My father started an affair with a blonde beauty called Olga, the secretary of the Left-bank Party Committee. Olga was better suited to the detached villa and to Father's lifestyle in general. My mother, faded and hysterical, did not fit in well with the bosses of a large industrial town.

Sometimes my sister and I went to visit Aunt Yudif, who lived in a mean, clay-walled house on the outskirts of town. She had nothing there. Water had to be carried from a well three streets away, and the draughty latrine was in the neighbouring yard, where goats grazed, pigs lazed, and the police chief's cow sadly flicked away the flies. The ruffians who lived on Yudif's street did not believe I was friendly with the divisional commander and could take them to the barracks, where we would be allowed to dismantle a machine-gun and ride on a machine-gun cart. When there were no grown-ups around, they used to shout 'Yid' at me and brandish knives in front of my nose.

Nadka, on the other hand, was not bothered by her Jewishness. She always made things seem better. She reconciled not only my mother and father, but also me with all the injustices of our life. The detached villa, for instance, the car, the servants, the imported electrical toys that were given to me by the City Party committee at the May Day and October Revolution celebrations . . . None of this was very fair: the other lads had neither maids nor cars, just shared flats. And at the holiday celebrations all they got were little bags of sticky sweets . . .

'What of it, Grishka,' Nadya would say, shrugging her round shoulders. 'It's just the way things are. Think yourself lucky!'

'But the others . . .'

'The others didn't suffer so much before the Revolution. Our mother was beaten up by the Tsarist police.'

'But she doesn't ride in Dad's car.'

'Look, what's Mum got to do with it? Don't you see: if everyone had the same, nobody would bother working, or studying. You are aware, Grishka, and you have to show people who are not aware what can be achieved if you don't spare yourself and work hard for the people.'

'But Mum . . .'

'Mum's a bit of a crackpot.'

And so we lived. I was annoyed that Pashet took Masha to the engineering workers' kindergarten by a different road, and was delighted whenever she went with her old grandfather, the old doctor, instead. Masha always brought him to our house.

Once when I was ill, I insisted that they call Doctor Tokar, my namesake, rather than the Party Committee's own physician.

'But he's got one foot in the grave. It would be better to call the village doctor,' my father grumbled in Ukrainian, which he considered closer to ordinary folk.

Doctor Tokar tapped my chest with his cold, bony fingers, and I enjoyed it: it was Masha's grandfather, after all.

'We have a sensitive young gentleman here,' said the doctor with a frown, turning not to my father or mother, but to Yudif. 'A drop of bromide would do no harm.'

'All these Tokars are the same,' my father laughed. 'I suppose you're related?'

'No, we're not related,' said the doctor, apparently offended.

My father gave a shudder, and I thought I heard him whisper: 'Counter . . .'

That night I cried, and Nadka came running into my room on tiptoes.

'Did the silly old man hurt you, Grishka? Ah, he doesn't understand . . . Grishka's fallen in love across the fence . . . But it's pure nonsense, of course – just a flash in the pan. Grishka will have lots of other girls!'

(Dear Nadka! In her distant land she does not know that to this day only Masha has been the joy and pain of my foolish fate . . .)

. . . My sister was chased after by a young poet called Yuz. People thought he came to our house to see me (I had also just begun to write verses). But Nadka's heart was lost to another – a handsome Muscovite, a favourite of Stalin, and an old friend of Mother's. He stayed with us once in 1936. I saw him with my sister in the store-room, where I was hiding my home-made bow and arrows. She was embracing him, and he had unbuttoned her dress and was touching her with his hands.

Autumn came, wet and slippery. I fell off my bicycle, bent the handlebars, and bruised my knee, and the bicycle ended up in the lumber-room before its time. My mother grew quite grey and looked like an old woman beside my father. They grew so far apart that they did not even quarrel any more, and at the end of November my father went to Moscow without her to vote for the new Constitution.

For three days my mother walked about the house with a terrible black expression, and then she suddenly also set off for the capital. What happened next was incomprehensible. My father telephoned endlessly from Moscow; then Nadka rushed off too, and Yudif moved into our villa.

Just before the first weekend in December there was a fall of snow, and in the evening there was a torchlight procession in honour of the Constitution. One column of marchers passed along our street – something that had never happened before. I peeped over the gate, and somebody handed me a burning pinewood torch.

'You'll set the house on fire!' screamed Yudif, and then burst into tears. 'My poor little orphan. Your mother is dead. Our Dora is gone. She poisoned herself because of that bandit Yakov . . .'

I remember my mother's funeral very clearly. It was preceded by tension and bustle in the house, with Aunt Yudif constantly arguing with the guard, Petya, the maid, the cook and the yard-keeper. Father had evidently decided to bury my mother quietly, without drawing attention to the circumstances of her death. But Yudif insisted on a splendid funeral. Through a half-open door I heard my aunt complaining to Mother's colleagues: 'He had her cremated on purpose: he wants to hush it all up . . . Nothing doing! Dora joined their set-up before he did. He was still being cosseted in the Jewish school when I was already taking her lunch to her at the office. If he doesn't want music, I'll order it myself!'

And so it was that the moment Father alighted from his train carriage he was deafened by a funeral march. He waved his hands in embarrassment at the musicians, telling them to end this disgraceful scene, but Yudif was also shouting: 'You didn't hire them! Play on, boys!' And the tiny woman ripped out of Nadka's hands the urn bearing an oval photograph of Mother.

The orchestra blew for all it was worth, and Mother's colleagues from the Education Commissariat lifted what remained of her on to a stretcher wrapped in red cloth, and the procession moved along the city's main street. Nadka and Yudif walked immediately behind the stretcher, while Father and I crawled along in the car at the very back. But suddenly, before we reached the Jewish cemetery, Father ordered the chauffeur to drive home.

'Never mind, my little orphan,' Aunt Yudif tried to console me in the evening. 'We'll often go and visit your mother. It's not far from my house. And we won't take *him* with us.' She nodded towards the half-open door of the study, where my father was packing a yellow travelling bag. 'The swine was ashamed because I buried Dora with her own folk. Well, he can lie with his own degenerate lot.'

It turned out to be a prophecy. The next morning Father left for a conference in Kiev, where he was arrested, and two days later we were thrown out of our villa and not even allowed to take our belongings. As a matter of fact, Yudif had long ago removed some of my mother's things to her miserable house – including even the Japanese bicycle. (In the spring, ashamed and triumphant, the old Tokars bought it for Masha.)

There was hardly room to turn in Aunt Yudif's hut. They rigged up a hammock for me at night, and my sister and aunt slept with their heads at opposite ends of the bed.

'Monsters!' Yudif sighed. 'They persecute their own people. Worse than Petlyura's lot.* Oh well, never mind . . . Don't cry, my orphan, I won't abandon you. We'll muddle through – especially with Nadka as helper . . .'

My aunt could not stop worrying about the fact that the Russian and Ukrainian papers, and also the local radio, had branded Father a corrupt enemy of the Party and people, mixed up with the Polish security services.

'And he got rid of Dora too, the monster,' Yudif added, but immediately fell silent, because the official cause of Mother's death was an oven door, and I can say with complete confidence that, whatever my father may have been like, my mother died an honest Bolshevik.

* The anti-Bolshevik, Ukrainian nationalist movement led by Simon Petlyura in the Civil War, 1918–20. [Tr.]

'The scum! He fell for that fancy Komsomol kid!' (That was what Yudif called Olga, although the latter was boss of a whole district, until her recent arrest.) 'Bloody Komsomol! But don't you be afraid, children. You are Tokars. That's right, Grishka, you're a Tokar, and you can forget your father's dirty Russian name.'

Yudif moved me from my old school to one on the outskirts, where lessons were a piece of cake, and I read everything I could lay my hands on, from *The Three Musketeers* to Sir Walter Scott – in short, anything that diverted me from our sorrowful existence.

As though by some wicked sorcery, our villa was transformed into a cramped little room, in which a treadle sewing machine rattled from morning until night, customers nattered, and enormous bloomers, girdles and brassieres piled up, taking all the mystery out of femininity. Everything changed – except Nadka! Nadka would cut short those women who chattered on too much, and did not bother to hiss at the lads who peeked into the toilet. ('OK, stare away you ninnies, if you find it interesting!') And she laughed when Yudif prodded her with her hump during the night. And she continued to spurn Yuz, who, scorning all fear, heroically courted the daughter of an enemy of the people.

(How I miss Nadka, and how I despise myself for not writing her letters, even though my work is not published in any case.)

My five years in the suburbs proved to be a difficult period in my life. I remember particularly well one unpleasant episode.

One spring, the Red Army was pitching tents beyond the Jewish cemetery, and the divisional commander's car often raced past our hut, spraying mud everywhere.

'Hey, Jewboy!' the local lads shouted to me once. 'Here comes your commander uncle. Go and introduce us to him!'

I went outside, feeling doomed, and, egged on by the mob, shouted: 'Uncle August! Hello, Uncle August!'

Swerving past a big blue puddle, the Ford slowly advanced on me. The canvas roof was folded back, and the stern commander was sitting there, quite motionless, as though posing for a photograph.

'Uncle August, it's me, Grisha . . .'

' " Uncle August", my foot!' jeered the boys, and I ran back inside, suppressing my tears. He used to sit me on his knee, and now he drove straight past me without even turning his head!

For a whole month I was consumed with anger and sorrow, as I went through all the possibilities of revenge in my mind. It was for that reason that I at once agreed – although we were outcasts – to go with Yuz to the May Day parade.

It rained during the night, and in the morning it was still drizzling when we arrived at the square and sat modestly at the end of the guest benches. I was shivering with cold and in earlier times would have started playing the fool. But now I was nine and a half, and in order to keep my mind on something serious I started criticizing the portraits displayed along the square.

'It's nothing like Stalin, and Marx's forehead is all wrong . . .'

But Yuz whispered to me reprovingly that we could discuss the merits of the paintings later.

A round little old soldier was strutting importantly along the assembled ranks pitilessly shortening the soldiers' greatcoats with a pair of scissors. I thought: this must be some mad whim of the divisional commander. After all, the longer their coats, the warmer the soldiers will be. 'Anyway, I'll pay you back,' I threatened the commander, eagerly awaiting his appearance on his bay mare, Helga.

Meanwhile the benches became packed with spectators. Yuz and I were squeezed from the left and right, and from behind by those without seats. The square burst into applause, and my father's successor appeared on the platform, accompanied by some other men, among whom I recognized only the bodyguard, Petya. But I was waiting not for them, but for the divisional commander. The road surface was wet, and I quietly murmured: 'Let him slip, let him slip . . .'

Yuz, not understanding what was wrong with me, was probably already regretting having brought me to the square.

A march sounded. The divisional commander rode out astride

Helga towards the brigade commander. His gloved hand was elegantly raised to his cap, and I entreated the horse to buck off my offender. I knew that to fall from a horse was a disgrace, but I did not think that it was also a bad omen. Especially now, when many people were being arrested. But in our family the worst that could happen had already happened.

I listened with hatred to Uncle August's falsetto voice, which I used to love, with its Baltic accent, as he greeted the rectangles of greatcoats, lopped off on his orders. The brigade commander rode alongside, and his horse seemed nervous. But Helga seemed to merge with the divisional commander in his long cavalry coat, which even covered his boots, and I realized that nothing would happen, because Uncle August had already reached the final column and congratulated them on the May Day festival, to which they had responded: 'Hurrah! Hurrah! Hurrah!'

And Helga did not even start, but merely shook her head picturesquely, like a circus horse. But then the divisional commander turned her round abruptly, and although thirty-six years have passed I remember to this day how Helga skidded over the cobblestones on all four hooves, as though on ice, and came to rest on her side just opposite our bench.

My heart leapt, and I immediately felt sorry for the divisional commander. Jumping up awkwardly, like a snared animal, he tried to free his foot from the stirrup. Two Red Army soldiers rushed to help Helga up. Uncle August cast them a casual nod, climbed into the saddle, and rode over to the platform with his hand held close to his cap-peak.

Yuz concluded that I was unwell (I had evidently turned green) and led me through the crowd of spectators to the park adjoining the square.

A month later the divisional commander was recalled to Moscow and shot together with Tukhachevsky.* The poet Yuz did not remain a free man for long either . . .

* Marshal M.N. Tukhachevsky, a brilliant Soviet military leader, shot in 1937 on trumped-up charges of 'treason' and 'espionage'. [Tr.]

What's so brilliant about all this? Cholyshev wondered. No, no, she shouldn't be over-exerting herself like that, hammering away on that typewriter like a young girl.

He raised his glasses and looked with pity at Zhenya's fingers with their clipped, unpainted nails. A working woman, he thought, with some resentment. Isn't Grishka ashamed to load her with work? It would be different if he'd written something worthwhile . . .

None the less, the old man had been disturbed by his son-in-law's memoirs, and he himself began to dig over the past in his mind.

He suddenly recalled one autumn day in 1914.

Returning from school, Pashka Cholyshev gulped down the simple lunch left for him by his mother, quickly did his homework, and the short September day seemed endless to him. There was nobody there to pull his ears, or send him to the shop for cigarettes, or next door to borrow a couple of roubles from Doctor Tokar's wife. And all because his brother Artem (because he was too smart, according to Mother!) had left the Mining Institute and volunteered for the army. Now he was probably in the training detachment, roaring out gypsy tunes with different words:

> For Holy Russia we'll boldly fight,
> And shed for her our youthful blood . . .

The war with the Germans had been in progress for a month and a half, and Pashka's mates were inciting him to abscond to the front line. He wouldn't be missed for some time, they said: he had no father (he had drowned), his brother was in the army, and his mother worked in the town council and was busy in the evenings too. An assistant notary was always hanging round her. They would probably get married soon. Of course, it wouldn't have been a bad thing to escape to the front from this town which, though a provincial capital, was a very dull place; but, to be honest, the war seemed as far away from here as America, to which no one from their street – for all their threats – had ever run away.

'Hey, Choly!' shouted Koska Drozd, seeing his friend. He was an even punier specimen than Pashka, and, true to his surname, which means thrush, was perched on a fence like a bird. 'A crowd of refugees has landed on the Jewish doctor!'

The neighbours' house was a little wealthier-looking: it was built of stone and even had a sand-pit. Doctor Aron Solomonovich Tokar, himself childless, had it made so that little children could play there without catching cold on the bare earth. All the mothers on Police Street thanked him kindly for this, but behind his back they expressed another opinion: 'The yid can't pull the wool over us orthodox folks' eyes. We know they bake matzos with children's blood. And the sly devil knows that when kids are sick their blood's thinner . . .'

This topic also caused arguments in the Cholyshev family. Artem insisted it was all lies and slander. His mother, Lyubov, frightened by the recent Beilis affair,* did not agree with him. Her brother Klim, a young priest, who was visiting them from the other riverbank, mocked her and took the side of his nephew.

But Lyubov would not listen to him: 'Are you behaving like a priest?' she complained. 'All the other priests are serious men, and all you can do is laugh and mock. You'd be better off playing the buffoon at fairgrounds instead of wailing in church.'

Pashka jumped over the fence to the neighbours' yard, but he could see no 'crowd of refugees', only a strange, chubby little girl messing about in the sand-pit, wearing a cambric dress, which was all wet.

'Who are you?' asked Pashka.

'Vonya . . .' said the little girl in a squealing voice.

'Certainly are!† What's up, have you no mummy? She's all mucky. She's peed herself.'

* M. Beilis, a Jew, was acquitted after a trial in Kiev in 1913, at which he was accused of the ritual murder of a Russian boy. [Tr.]
† 'Vonya' is similar to the Russian for 'a nasty smell'. [Tr.]

'Vonya, Vonya!' babbled the girl, and angrily swung her little shovel.

'She's got a temper,' said Koska Drozd. 'OK, Vonya-Bonya, shout for your mum. You'll get cold.'

'Come on, let's go,' said Pashka, making a face.

He immediately lost interest in the refugees. The doctor had a bathtub with fancy-shaped legs at home, and they didn't even give the kid a bath. The Cholyshevs had to fetch water from a well, but if their mother caught them with dirty necks . . .

'Mummy, Mummy!' the little girl started whimpering.

The back door opened, and into the neat little porch stepped . . . not a girl, not a woman – but rather, an angel! A long Madonna-like face, green eyes, a high bosom, slender waist, and curving hips. She looked no older than the girls in the top form at school, but she had something that schoolgirls did not even dream of. Pashka and Koska gaped in wonder.

Youthful, bathed in the autumn sunlight, the boys would remember for the rest of their lives how she carefully walked down those steps.

As if she was testing water with her foot, thought Pashka.

The woman's stained silk dress smelt of something sinful, as well as perfume.

'Mummy! Mummy' shrieked the little girl, but the refugee, lifting her hems, crept across the yard hoping she would not be noticed.

'Mummy!' whined the girl, as though guessing that the woman was hurrying off somewhere where the girl would be a hindrance to her.

'What's the matter, my child?' said the refugee in Polish, floating over to her after all. 'I don't have time . . . Shhh! Mother of God!'

She lifted the girl by the scrag of her neck, dragged her over to the porch and, screwing up her face, smacked her wet backside. But the girl for some reason did not start crying, but started crawling up the steps.

'They're not Jews,' said Koska Drozd.

Pashka nodded in agreement. Jews didn't wallop their children, nor did they recognize the Mother of God, although the Virgin Mary was Jewish.

'No, no, we are Jews, boy, we are,' said the woman ingratiatingly.

She's scared the doctor's wife will drive her out, thought Pashka.

And suddenly, as though addressing an adult, the beautiful woman gave a smile full of promise and said: 'I'll be seeing you, lad!'

Like a fleeting vision she disappeared behind the gate, and a cloud of her strange smell, mingled with scent, floated away in the autumn breeze.

Pashka went to bed early that evening. His mother had not come home. She was probably at the cinema again with her notary. Pashka was beginning to nod off, when suddenly the refugee took him by the hand and asked him, in front of all the youngsters, if he could row her across the river. Why this was necessary, Pashka could not understand (there was a stone bridge!), but he said he could, even though he was afraid of going on the river since his father's death.

And so he led the refugee out on to Police Street, and all the boys, including Koska, gazed after them as though bewitched. Pashka did not have a boat. Klim did, but he lived on the other bank, about three miles downriver. None the less Pasha and the woman found themselves in a boat. He handled the oars and she sat at the stern, in silence, because Pashka did not know how to start conversations. But suddenly the beautiful woman confessed that she didn't really want to cross the river at all. She just wanted to be alone with Pashka. Here, on the autumnal water, nobody would disturb them, whereas on either bank there were many bad people.

That was what she said to Pashka, in Russian; but he was afraid to leave the oars and move over to her at the stern. There was a strong wind on the river. The boat could easily overturn. It was so cold his teeth ached, and when he awoke Pashka noticed he had not closed the shutters.

Groaning as he no longer groaned today, Cholyshev threw his black school coat over his nightshirt and crept out of the house in unlaced shoes. Everyone in the vicinity was asleep, but there was a strip of light coming from the doctor's kitchen. In the porch, next to the tall thin doctor, was standing a policeman.

'Please try and find her,' the doctor was saying. 'My wife and I will be very grateful.'

'Where can we look now? Trains pass through the station every hour – and on top of all that there are all the troop trains. You ought to have alerted us earlier.'

'My wife telephoned the police station.'

The doctor had the same kind of telephone at home as Pashka's mother had at the council. The Cholyshevs also had their own telephone while their father – before his building business went bankrupt – was renting a large, seven-roomed flat.

'A telephone isn't a piece of paper. You can't put your signature on it. You should have submitted an application, and attached a picture.'

'We don't have a photograph. She ran away in a hurry.'

'And, er, in what way is the missing person related to you?'

'She's a distant relative . . .' replied the doctor uncertainly.

'She's not a crook, by any chance, is she? Leaves the child . . . then skedaddles . . . Are we supposed to search every station in the empire? Take the little girl to an orphanage, Doctor, that's my advice. Haven't you got enough relations? They'll have her christened there, and you won't be inconvenienced with her at all . . .'

But within a day it turned out that the refugee had not been thinking of deserting the child after all. She was merely hurrying to a rendezvous. An officer was waiting for her in an hotel. They had probably met in a train, or at the railway junction to which she had fled from her village in the border area. Perhaps she herself was of an amorous disposition, or perhaps the officer turned her head, but whatever the reason, she went off to the hotel on her own. The hotel servant made a mental note of her, but after all, there is no law against a girl visiting a soldier.

In the morning, another boots noticed a draught coming from under the door of room twenty-three. There had been a change in the weather overnight, and it had started raining. The guest had probably had a drop too much to drink and had forgotten to close the window: he would catch cold.

The boots knocked on the door but there was no reply. Then he went down to the office, and he and a clerk went out to the inner yard together. The window of room twenty-three was wide open, and in the withered flower-bed below there were fresh footprints, not yet washed away by the rain.

'Call the police,' said the clerk with a sigh, and the boots ran off. They broke the door in. The beautiful young woman was lying on the iron bedstead, naked, with a stocking round her neck. Her stomach and thighs were covered with blood. The inquest established that the maniac had slashed his poor victim with a sword and then wiped the blade on her ragged dress, which was lying on the rug.

That was what was written in the local newspapers, and for a long time after Pashka dreamt of the beautiful refugee – not naked, it is true, but always covered in blood. He even convinced himself that beauty must always be accompanied by the horror of murder and mystery. This horror remained in Cholyshev for a long time, perhaps for ever, and thirty, forty, even fifty years later he feared that someone would slit his daughter's throat.

Meanwhile, Artem was made an ensign. He was awarded one George Cross, then another, but their mother still did not get married. Then suddenly the battalion commander personally informed her that her son, Artem Rodionovich Cholyshev, had fallen. Lyubov Simonovna said nothing, and carried on working at the town council, but her notary no longer spent long evenings at their house. And one day Pashka saw that his mother was not young any more, and not at all stern.

Unexpectedly, on the first autumn holiday, she wheeled a real, though not new, bicycle into the yard, holding it by the handlebars like a goat by the horns. Her eyes were watchful, as though she were afraid that her second son would also run off to the war. For a month Pashka raced all over town on his bicycle. But then in a suburban back alley some boys knocked him off, pierced the tyres, tore out the spokes, and broke the gears. Pashka fought them off with the pump, and when they snatched that from him he smashed two of the lads' noses with the edge of his hand, and dragged the crippled bicycle back to Police Street. He felt ashamed in front of his mother, but reckoning that he had fathomed the laws of human envy, he was angry not with the boys but with his mother and himself.

'Go on, whip me!' he said. 'I'm not afraid of your belt. You should be glad I'm still alive. Though, if they'd killed me, I'd have deserved it. It's nothing to swank about. A bicycle's above our station!'

'Oh, you old man,' said his mother in surprise. 'What a wise old philosopher you are, Pashka . . .'

Then she tried cooking a tasty meal each evening to keep him at home. But Pashka wasn't interested. Let her drink port or Cahors on the sly if she wanted to, and then wag her tongue in the porch with the neighbours, as if she were the same as them . . . These were boring times. The only thing that livened them up was when the Tsar drove through the town on his way to the miliary HQ, and even then there were so many Cossacks round his car that it was impossible to see him.

But then in March the students were involved in skirmishes with the police, set fire to the police station, and total freedom was proclaimed. They all put on red arm-bands, and guttural, often ill-educated voices shouted from street-benches and soap-boxes at meetings big and small.

'The town's been taken over by Jews,' Klim complained to his nephew.

'Don't you like them?' asked Pashka with a wink.

'I can't pretend I do. Of course, they're the Lord's chosen people. One mustn't treat them badly. But I don't see any reason to love them, either.'

'You're not a Black Hundreder, are you?'*

'God forbid.'

'They say that from the autumn they'll be admitted to the college over and above the quota.'

'Quite right . . .'

'I know it is,' Pashka agreed, 'but people don't like them.'

'They don't like anyone,' said Klim.

'No, it's different with the Jews.'

'You are right, of course,' Klim sighed. 'Anti-Semitism is certainly a sin, but I'm afraid there must be some reason why it is so ingrained. Russia, you see, lagged so far behind the rest of Europe that even in the last century (or in some cases even four centuries ago) some clever people hit upon the idea that it wasn't so much that Russia was slow in becoming enlightened, but rather that Europe had rushed head-over-heels to the Devil. So the Russians were farther from the Devil, and therefore closer to God. In other words, *they* are the chosen people. But in the Holy Scriptures there's not so much as a word about the Russians . . . Christ came down to Earth not here, you see, but in Jewish lands, and it was the Jews, not us, that he taught and fed with loaves. He didn't even think about the Russians. True enough, there was no such thing as the Slavic lands at that time, but it's still a pity. He could have waited a few hundred years and been born, say, in a Russian wooden hut with a smoky stove. Nobody would have turned the little babe out into the frost . . . They would have given him shelter and kindness. So you see, if you look at it closely,

*The Black Hundreds were a group of extreme reactionary, anti-Semitic thugs, involved in the pogroms of the early twentieth century and encouraged by the last Tsar to attack 'revolutionaries' of all shades. [Tr.]

31

hatred of the Jews is a sublime, religious hatred. And though it seems unenlightened to call someone a "bloody Jew", in fact there's a deeper meaning behind it: "It's not you who are the chosen people, but us!" And then again, the Jews are skinflints: they lend money for profit, and amass capital. Your father – God rest his soul – was Siberian through and through, and he went bankrupt, but a Jew in his position would have survived. So you see, there are different kinds of hatred of the Jews. There's a mean, everyday, frivolous hatred – the same way as people don't like Greeks, Armenians, or Tatars. But there's also a higher kind of hatred – a mystical anti-Semitism. That's a very different matter.'

'But do you believe that God chose them?' asked Pashka.

'That I don't know. Perhaps the Lord did choose them, but in their conceit they refused to accept His Son.'

'But if the Jews had recognized Christ, it wouldn't have made things any easier for the Russians,' said Pashka timidly.

Klim stared at his nephew in surprise, then spat, and gave a loud laugh: 'What are you thinking of! *If* they had recognized Him! The whole of history would have been different if they had accepted Jesus! The Saviour without Golgotha! What would have become of the Church? It's terrible to think of it: these are hard enough times for it as it is! Oh, Pashka, there is trouble in the air, and I, a spiritual shepherd, am planting cabbages like a Roman commander.* I see no light through the cataracts on my eyes. How can I lead people? A couple of days ago a young lady came to me, a Jewess. She was shaking all over. "I want to be christened," she said. "But why?" I asked. Before, it was obvious – they couldn't enter university without it. But she gave no explanation: I want to, and that's all . . . Eventually I got her to confide in me. She said she was afraid of the Revolution. She was afraid of her own kinsmen, her brothers and cousins. "You oppressed them too much," she said to me. "You helped in the pogroms." "I didn't help," I said.

*A reference to the Roman emperor Diocletian's celebrated *bon mot* about happiness consisting more in planting cabbages than in the pursuit of power. [Tr.]

"I don't mean you,' she replied. In a word, one gives as good as one gets. "There will be no holding them back now," she said. "Once they break loose . . ." And so she came running to me to be saved. But what am I – forgive me, Christ – a saviour, and defender against the Revolution? I didn't love the Tsar myself, I must admit; many's the time I've cursed him over a glass of vodka and drunk with your father and brother to the coming of the radiant future. And I'm still not certain whether these disturbances are for the good or the beginnings of a catastrophe. I tried to dissuade that young Jewess. Wait a while, I said, and see how things turn out. Baptism is a serious step . . . But she'd have none of it! She wanted it that minute – the sooner the better. So I baptized her – without any enjoyment – and was possessed by the evil thought that our Church wouldn't last much longer if that's the kind who are taking refuge in it. What would happen if a hundred thousand of them turned to the Orthodox Church?! They may not discriminate between Greeks and Jews in the Kingdom of God, but down here there's a big difference. The Jews have got different blood – it's too hot and impatient, and not ready for submission. Just you see if they wouldn't infect our good, quiet, sublime Church with their indignant rationality, and turn the cathedrals into halls for political meetings, or synagogues . . .'

Meanwhile the year 1917 ended in total confusion. Pashka's mother was drinking, and Klim was depressed and suddenly in winter broke with religion. He moved out of his large priest's house into a shed which he somehow contrived to make habitable. Pashka missed classes at the school because half of the teachers, not recognizing the new government, were also missing. Indeed, the new government itself did not last long to begin with. First one set of troops would drop into town, then another. No one moved in with Cholyshevs, but Doctor Tokar's house was popular because it had a telephone, water-closet and running water. The plumbing, it is true, immediately went on strike, but the telephone went on working for some reason, luring all the regular and irregular gangs passing through the town. The Devil knows what the house would have ended up like if the doctor had not finally severed the telephone wires.

This period of history – later for some reason declared 'heroic' – seemed terribly dreary to the young Cholyshev, and when in later years his daughter asked him about the Civil War he could not recall anything particularly outstanding. One thing only: he got a leaving certificate from the school and entered the Mining Institute.

But Klim did not take to the bottle. He kept himself busy in his garden. Then, suddenly, the following summer he volunteered for Denikin's White Army and went off with them. Dressed up strangely in a field-shirt, breeches and leggings, he called on the Cholyshevs to say goodbye.

Lyubov Simonovna was amazed: 'What are you doing it for?'

'I'm tired of all these boors, Lyuba.'

'What do you think you are, Citizen Kornienko? A prince?'

'Of course we're not gentry, but we knew our place. Whereas nowadays there's riff-raff crawling out of every hole. They shouted for joy because they had freedom, and now they want to lord it so that there's no freedom left at all.'

'The Jews, you mean?'

'The Jews, and the Russians, and our Ukrainian lot . . . they're all in it,' Klim sighed. 'You wouldn't believe it, Lyuba, but the Red Army's full of the same people who were most active in the pogroms. They don't care who they go in with – so long as they can climb a little higher than the rest! And now they've covered the country in blood . . .'

'And what are the White officers doing?!' Pashka interrupted.

'At least they are defending what belonged to them – Holy Russia. It's a doomed cause, of course, but understandable. However you look at it, it's all their own . . . The Red commissars haven't even composed their own song yet: they just changed the words of an old cadets' song and roar out: "We'll die in battle together for *this* . . ." What *this* is, you'd better not ask. For such inquisitiveness they'll smash your skull against a cellar wall. Freedom! Our own power! Huh! If that's our own, I'd rather have somebody else's. Because when we used to have somebody else's, a poor person had a lot more room. It's our own fault. We didn't look after what we had – and lost it . . . I lived badly. We all did . . . And then in my haste and impatience I even tore the cross from my breast, without really thinking about it. And so I led that lot into temptation . . . There's only one thing to do – left! right! about turn!'

'You put it well,' said Lyubov Simonovna with a sigh. 'Do you at least believe you can defeat the Reds?'

'If I believed that, I'd take Pashka with me.' Klim put his arm round his nephew. 'No, I don't foresee victory. For victory we should have been pious in the past. So there will be no victory – just a last parade, and my place will be among the fallen . . . But let Pashka stay at home. He hasn't sinned before Russia yet.'

Then came the autumn of 1919. Rainy. Cold. Tedious. And there was no food, although Cholyshev now had his first earnings – from making playing cards. Without hurrying he could produce a whole pack in three or four evenings. He did use up a great deal of kerosene, though.

Pashka was sitting in his room, and in his mother's room Klim's wife, Leokadia, was complaining: 'You Kornienkos are a bad lot . . .'

Since her husband left, Leokadia had started visiting her sister-in-law often.

'That's enough,' replied Lyubov Simonovna indifferently. 'If you'd nagged him less, he wouldn't have gone.'

'Nagged him? It's not that. You Kornienkos never could settle down.'

'Why bring me into it? I'm still here.'

'Huh, who needs you now, you old crow? Otherwise you'd be up and off too . . .'

'Nobody. Nobody needs either of us. Here, taste this . . .'

Since port had disappeared, Pashka's mother was not averse to home-distilled vodka.

'I don't want that poison. I'm going. It's dark already.'

'Stay for the night.'

'And where would I be if they set my house on fire?'

'Who could possibly have his eye on that?'

'You'd be surprised. There was a bunch of them on the bridge this morning. Looked like your Ukrainians, and sailors. Tell Pashka to accompany me home.'

'Certainly not. You think more of that shed of yours than of me and my son. What if they shoot him?'

'They won't shoot him. Will you see me home, Pashka?' she asked, going into Cholyshev's room.

He quickly covered the queen of diamonds with a piece of paper in embarrassment. She had turned out round-faced and large-breasted, exactly like his aunt. This surprised him. Before, when he had spent the night at Klim's and Leokadia had walked about with her hair down, wearing only a linen nightdress, Pashka had not noticed her. At that time he was preoccupied with thoughts of man's main purpose in life, and of how to make sure one did not *miss* it. But Klim, gloomy and dissatisfied after unfrocking himself, answered reluctantly: 'It's time you got some girls into trouble. It's a sin, of course . . . But without a little sin like that, you could end up committing a bigger one. Don't be a fool, lad. That "main purpose" is like a mirage – you think it's just in front of you, and when you go up to it it dashes off, leaving you to run after it again. There is no main purpose. It used to be God, but now . . . I don't know what it is . . .'

'A woman is asking you to accompany her home. Will you really refuse?' said Leokadia, and Pashka followed her out into the damp November darkness. Walking beside his aunt he reflected that while there was a demand for them he would make another couple of dozen packs of cards, and then, perhaps, a job might turn up in the district drawing office. These crazy times had to come to an end some time . . . But his thoughts about the future were just as inconsequential as his thoughts about cards. He again remembered the murdered refugee woman in the hotel. She – even if only for herself – felt that Main Thing. She was drunk. And happy. She chucked everything, ran away from everyone. So she must have had a reason . . . Here they were, Leokadia and Pashka, walking through the deserted town at night. Suddenly they heard hooves. Some patrol or other, from boredom or foolhardiness, was about to shoot down the last in the line of Cholyshevs, and you would never know whether there was any Meaning invested in you. You hadn't even finished painting the cards . . .

The clatter of hooves came nearer. Pashka felt afraid, but also curious, as though the noise of the hooves was about to reveal some secret. On his left was a warm woman, on his right – coldness and loneliness. It was from there that the horsemen were approaching.

'Holy Mother of God,' whispered Leokadia and clung to Pashka's arm. The patrol rode past. In the darkness the horses looked incredibly big, and the riders very small. They were hunched up, and bouncing in the saddles like corpses.

'It's over,' sighed the ex-priest's wife, but did not let go of Pashka, and he was surprised: she was not a large woman, though round, but in the dark she seemed big.

'We must get over the bridge quickly . . .' she whispered, although it was quiet all around. There was only the rain and the night.

'We'll soon be over it,' Pashka mumbled.

Leokadia's tenseness transmitted itself to him, and he felt afraid to move away from her. On the contrary, he wanted to press up against her, or into her, or even hide in her. No, this wasn't the Main Thing, but it teased him and pushed everything else into the background – the Mining Institute, the unfinished pack of cards, even the murdered refugee . . . He thought: if they shoot me now, my life will have been a meaningless stump, without purpose and mystery.

There were no sentries on the other side. Pashka and his aunt walked round the graveyard and up to the shed. Leokadia took off the padlock and opened the door, and the pure scent of wormwood wafted out of the darkness. Pashka was glad that there was no candle under the icon. That was one eye less. It was not God he was afraid of, but Klim, as though it was Klim who was peeping out of the corner.

'Go on. I've made the bed . . .' said a voice in the darkness at last, and Pashka, as though he were at home on Police Street, as though this happened every evening, pulled off his boots and clothes and lay down under the blanket on the right side of the bed, where Klim used to lie.

The smell of sin was thick and enveloping, like the scent of hay or a cloud.

'Oh, don't show them to Lyubov!' exclaimed Aunt Leokadia, clapping her hands together. 'Ooh, what bruises . . .'

And Pashka Cholyshev carried those bruises under his jacket through the chill November morning like a young warrior his first scars.

That evening his mother said nothing, and Pashka, after a hurried bit to eat, sat down to complete his pack of cards. He soon felt sleepy, but in the middle of the night it was as if he had been struck by lightning: he jumped up and dressed without lighting a lamp, left a note with some lie or other, and sped off through the dark and eerie streets.

'Oh, Pashecka, my darling! I've given you a taste . . .' whispered the woman, and Pashka was both joyful and angry, he suffered and tormented himself, feeling he was falling and sinking, as though disappearing under ice.

'Move in with her,' said Lyubov Simonovna at the end of the second week. Pashka was bent over a drawing. His hands and shoulders were shaking, and his knees were aching. He must have caught a chill.

'Go and live with her,' his mother repeated, 'or you'll get consumption from all that running about. And you can't eat properly these days . . .'

Pashka tumbled on to his bed, his stomach churning as though he had drunk home-made vodka. The oil-lamp spun round the room like a huge butterfly, and when Pashka made a determined effort to focus on it, a pain shot through the back of his neck and his eyes swelled up as though they would burst.

'Mum . . .' he breathed, and lost consciousness.

Coming to during the night, he noticed that his father's watch had fallen out of his trouser-pocket and was showing a quarter past two. So he could still reach Leokadia's while it was still dark. But, while bending over his boots, Pashka knocked over his drawing board, and he regained consciousness only eight days later, in December.

Outside the window it was winter. There was snow on the trees. Pashka felt light and comfortable. And the snow seemed like a dream . . . But still he grew tired of gazing at the whiteness, and called out: 'Mum!'

Leokadia came in instead of his mother.

'Are you better?' she smiled, sitting down on the bed. 'Your fever is down . . .' His aunt placed her palm on his brow. The ends of her fingers felt strange.

'Is it prickly?' she asked. 'I shaved you.'

'What for?'

'Because you have typhus, Pashka. I shaved you all over. Now you're like a little baby . . .'

Pashka was afraid his mother would hear, and asked in a whisper where she was. Leokadia paused, but then, evidently with great effort, said: 'She's in hospital. She's got typhus too.'

'I'll go and see her.'

Pashka tried to rise, but his aunt pressed him to the pillow. And he himself felt so weak and light that it seemed he would float away if he went outside.

'You're lying. She's dead . . .'

In the daylight he felt embarrassed to address Leokadia familiarly as *ty*, or 'thou'. He felt like crying, and the shaved parts of his body were unpleasantly itchy. 'She's dead,' he repeated, looking for pity. But his aunt said nothing.

In the evening Doctor Tokar appeared.

'Tell him where Lyuba is, Doctor,' said Leokadia. 'He doesn't believe she's in hospital.'

'She is in hospital,' repeated Doctor Tokar with displeasure.

'How is she?'

'The same as you were recently. Don't you remember?' said the doctor with a frown.

Pashka lay in bed for a week, scarcely thinking of his mother. But when Leokadia went briefly to her house on the left bank, he suddenly jumped out of bed, pulled on his clothes, which felt strange after being sterilized, and dragged himself to the nearest hospital. The youth at the reception desk, evidently a medical student mobilized to help deal with the typhus outbreak, leafed through a pile of papers and replied that nobody by the name of Cholyshev, Lyubov Simonovna, born 1874, had been admitted in the last month. Other hospitals said the same thing.

Back home Pashka wept and castigated Leokadia: 'You destroyed her . . .'

'How can you say such a thing!' his aunt took fright, and in turn attacked Pashka: 'It's you who destroyed her. It was your louse . . .'

In the morning Cholyshev forced himself to walk to the barracks on the outskirts where, as he was told at the hospitals, those who died of typhus were taken. The guard lazily chased Pashka away, but he hung around and eventually managed to get into the mortuary. The bodies were piled up – naked ones with partially clothed ones, men with women.

'I must find my mother,' Pashka explained to the porters who were carrying about the bodies and throwing them on to a cart.

'Go and rummage about a bit, you might find her,' joked a drunk fellow, and Pashka obediently pulled at the feet of a yellow female body covered in big brown patches. (Like a skewbald horse, he thought automatically.)

His mother was not there. But Cholyshev trudged every day to the morgue, and, if he didn't exactly make friends with the carters, at least drank moonshine with them in a little partitioned-off room. It was warm there, with a stove puffing away, and the men's foul language did not bother Pashka. He was numbed to it, and forgot all other words except 'yes' and 'no'.

'Oh, you old man! What a wise old philosopher you are, Pashka!' His mother's words kept recurring to him, filled now with new meaning: 'How strange you are!', or 'How hard-hearted you are!', or 'You don't love me, Pashka!'

'I do love you!' he felt like shouting out in the warm little room, but his voice retreated inside him and jarred against his ribs. He did not know where his mother was, but he guessed that she was lonely. Here he was boozing with the lads, and she had nothing to drink. If only he could find her and give her a decent burial, and then come to her grave in the spring and whisper: 'Mother . . .'

I should have thought of that earlier, he chastised himself. Before she started drinking, when she believed that I would grow up to be her support and comfort. Before I did her the favour of running off to her sister-in-law . . .

'Come and join us for good!' said one of the elderly carters with a wry smile. 'So long as there's a spot of typhus and hunger around, there's plenty to do. You'll have a full belly, and even save up for the future.'

Cholyshev grew gloomy at the thought of the future. He went back to the Mining Institute, and a year later also got a construction job. There were two of them now: Leokadia had moved in with him, and looked after the house. Not a word was heard of Klim, though the turmoil had died down. Either he was killed, or else went abroad with the White Army and found himself another woman, leaving Leokadia and Pashka to torment each other. It had long been an open secret on Police Street that they were not living together just as aunt and nephew. The women were sorry for

41

Pashka. He was young: it was a girl he needed, not a husbandless old woman . . . But the girl had not grown up yet! Adopted by the Tokars, she would walk along sedately in lace and ribbons, between the doctor and his wife, but would pull faces whenever she met Cholyshev.

'Bronka, leave the young man in peace. Pashka, pay no attention,' the Tokars would blush. Being childless themselves, they grew attached to the little girl and forgave her everything, and she was able to twist them round her little finger. When she discovered from the neighbours that she was adopted, Bronka would sometimes call herself by her Polish name – Barbara – and sometimes in Russian – Varka.

It was not Bronka, however, who occupied Pavel's thoughts. He was worried by something else: his young life was not a happy one. At the building site and at the institute people looked at him like a stranger. Pavel himself could not understand why he was so quiet and so down in the dumps. Perhaps it was the chain of misfortunes, or his loveless life with Leokadia that finished him. He certainly was not burning with revolutionary enthusiasm. The monotonous raptures of the crowd, herded together, offended him. He instinctively held himself back from all cells and meetings, afraid of losing himself among others. He was only dimly aware of his own identity, but none the less he steered clear of imposed opinions, as though they could fall on him like bricks from a scaffold and smash his skull.

Even in the days when leaders mixed directly with the masses, Cholyshev shunned all forms of Soviet pomp, and Leon Trotsky himself awoke no interest in the victory of the proletarian cause in him.

In the spring of 1923, paying homage to the region's working class and students, the People's Commissar for Military Affairs dropped into Pavel's town for a day. At the Mining Institute Cholyshev was not given a ticket for the leader's meeting, but at work, where he had risen to become an assistant foreman, he was entered in the general list. The former merchants' hall was packed an hour and a half before the meeting began. Not wishing to bump into the institute activists, Pavel climbed to the very top gallery. I might as well see what he's about, he thought. He *is* an idol, after all.

The sound of applause and heart-rending cries of 'Long Live the leader of the Red front!', 'Long live the leader of the world revolution!', and 'Three cheers for the great people's leader of the Red Army!' the People's Commissar for Military Affairs was carried aloft by Komsomol girls on to the stage and carefully set down at a long table covered with red cloth. To Pavel's surprise, Trotsky was in civvies. He looked tired and sullen. His broad forehead hung over the lower part of his face. Not surprising, since it was after one o'clock in the morning, and Trotsky had already performed before the military, the railwaymen, the metalworkers, and the regional Party committee.

'Comrades, I call upon the chairman of the construction board,' said the secretary of the Mining Institute's Party cell, who was sitting next to the leader.

'We want Trotsky! We want Trotsky!' roared the hall.

'Quiet, please, comrades,' said the secretary, raising his arm. 'Comrade Trotsky will speak in a moment. But first you, Comrade Dembo . . .'

A diminutive fellow in glasses, shaking all over but none the less preening himself, leapt on to the rostrum. He took a piece of paper from his breast pocket and in a loud voice, losing the place in his excitement, read out: 'Minutes of extraordinary meeting of the rates and disputes commission of construction board number one. It was decreed: "To enrol Comrade Trotsky as an honorary painter of the first construction board and, with effect from the twelfth day of April 1923, to pay him a class-seven rate of tariff, in conformity with the tariffs of the Union of Builders." '

The hall again shook to roars of 'Hurrah!' and greetings to the 'iron leader', the 'world leader' and the 'people's Red leader', but Trotsky did not even smile.

He's used to it, Pavel thought.

'I now call upon . . .' That was as much as the Party secretary managed to say, before the hall erupted into a roar which went on for one minute, two minutes, ten minutes . . . Now only the People's Commissar for Military Affairs could calm them, and this he did by stepping up to the rostrum. The 'iron leader's' movements were practised. Making a speech was clearly no more difficult for him than blowing his nose.

Having tossed out a few winged phrases about the selflessness and enthusiasm of youth, Trotsky went on to stun everyone by announcing that the United Soviet States was a poor country – thirty-six times poorer than the American United States. The capitalists could buy up the whole country. In a single year they would ruin the whole of our nationalized industry if we did not bristle up and declare a monopoly on foreign trade as a barrier. The whole hall froze with fear, and Trotsky called on us in his truly iron voice to work and spare no effort, and to spare no effort and work. And to economize.

'We must perform miracles of heroism,' Trotsky shouted. 'Just as the small exploiter and petty proprietor used to. He did not spare himself, nor his wife or children, he slept only four hours a day, counted every kopeck, but in return there was the period of primitive accumulation of capital. And we must struggle with the same passion, but for our Soviet, socialist kopeck! And then, despite our pitiful, shameful poverty, we shall pull the country out of its destitution and not yield to capital!'

The hall rocked with the ovation, but Pavel felt sad and lonely. He squeezed through the crowd to an emergency exit. He did not want to meet his fellow students, who would inundate him with questions about how he had found Trotsky. And how could he tell the truth?

But the crowd from upstairs overtook him, and he went into the smoking-room to wait until the enthusiasm died down and the Komsomol activists dispersed to their hostels. A quarter of an hour later, however, when he looked out at the spiral staircase, he saw that the lower steps were littered with boys and girls in jackets and leather coats, like flies, and in front of them stood the people's leader.

'Comrade Trotsky, are you not afraid to speak in front of so many people?' asked one lad.

'Why? Would you be?' said Trotsky in a surprised voice.

'You bet!'

'Are two hundred people frightening?'

'Two hundred! Even twenty . . .'

'What about five?

'Well, five wouldn't be so bad . . .'

'In that case, convince yourself that there are not two hundred or one thousand two hundred in the hall, but only one person – and he's a fool,' Trotsky smiled.

They all burst out laughing, but Pavel was taken aback: He doesn't regard us as people, he thought. But then, he has power behind him. Klim once said that Trotsky used machine-guns to turn back Red Army troops who were deserting. He drew them up in ranks, shot every tenth man, and drove the rest back to fight the Czechs. Here he knows he doesn't need to resort to machine-guns . . .

That's the way it is, Klim – Cholyshev found himself addressing his missing uncle. All around there is jubilation, but I feel sick. Perhaps I'm really a bit of a crank? What do you say, you bloody émigré?'

'You're stupid,' replied Klim suddenly from wherever he was. 'You're stupid . . . Why do you doubt when it is as clear as daylight: they are the fools, not you. Because you think for yourself, while they think in a herd.'

The spiral staircase was still digesting the reply of the People's Commissar for Military Affairs, while in the doorway of the smoking-room, just as once before in the garden, Klim tried to make Pavel listen to reason: 'You should be glad, my boy, that they haven't conquered you yet, that you are still yourself. Do you remember how they hoped to find ten righteous men? "For the sake of the ten I will not destroy this town." Well, righteous men disappeared long ago. But if just ten sinners could be found, each one thinking for himself, then the city – and the State – would not perish. You see . . . And yet you are ashamed and sickly, like some frail little girl. Lift up your head . . .' said Klim, then vanished.

Pavel went out on to the stairs, looked again at the iron leader, and thought: It's easy enough to joke when you're in favour. They'll cheer you for any stupid – or vile – remark you make.

And later, when Trotsky was outwitted, and they first took away his machine-guns and then exiled him to the back of beyond, Pavel, though he felt sorry for the poor iron leader, nevertheless remembered his midnight meeting with him.

Zhenya tapped away at her typewriter, and the pile of typed pages grew, but she did not manage to give herself up entirely to the work. Pashet disturbed her. Having read through the first portion he did not, for some reason, ask for the next.

Does he really not find it interesting? Zhenya wondered. Or is he just pretending? No, he has just convinced himself that Tokarev is untalented. And since I said the manuscript showed talent, I have to be taught a lesson. Lord, when will this family struggle of ours end? When one of us dies . . .

She suddenly drew herself up, wondering if she had spoken that last thought aloud.

Hmm . . . Happy people don't torment each other. Their careers use up all their energy. But we are failures . . . So what if he doesn't want to read it? Perhaps it's for the best – there are those rather unpleasant pages about Varvara Alekseyevna coming up. I still can't fathom what there was about that witch that attracted Pashet. Poor soul, he didn't have much luck with wives . . .

At the age of sixteen Varvara – or Bronka – Tokar looked twenty and was almost as tall as Cholyshev.

'It's awful! What's happening to the girl? You'll see, nothing good will come of it!' said Aron Solomonovich with a sigh.

Cholyshev and the old doctor were sitting in the shade of an awning in a boulevard. Pavel was drinking beer; the doctor was eating ice cream.

'There's no rest with your Bronka,' complained the young engineer. 'When ladies come to see me, that little hussy perches on the fence and roars the filthiest words imaginable at them. Now she's started throwing stones. Can't you give her a sedative?'

'Pavel, medicine is powerless in this instance,' said Doctor Tokar with a timid smile. 'You'll have to help yourself. You're still young. Why are you ruining yourself in this country of ours?! And why aren't you at work, by the way? They haven't given you the sack, have they?'

'No, I'm on holiday.'

'Thank goodness. You gave me a shock there! Do you know what I would say to you? Go away! Yes, yes, leave! Nobody's keeping you here now . . .'

'I know.'

Pavel blushed, realizing that the doctor was alluding to Leokadia. Two years earlier Klim had turned up out of the blue in the Kingdom of Serbs, Croats and Slovenes (as Yugoslavia was then known) and started to inundate his wife with messages. Living in a strange country, he wrote, was not sweet, but nor was living apart. Leokadia haunted the thresholds of the district's most serious institutions, and, emphasizing the fact that she had no family or home, and was not working, she bought with her tears an exit visa.

'You should leave, Pasha. There will only be unpleasantness for you in this God-forsaken place. Go to Moscow. Here, you're just drifting, and that will end badly, believe me. I'm an old man. I also committed the colossal stupidity of not leaving. Of course, it wasn't easy – because of the war. We intended to leave, but somehow never got going. And yet we could have settled in Rostov, in Tiflis, or on the Volga, in Saratov, for instance. There was no Pale of Settlement for doctors. The girl would never have found out who she was and would have grown up quite different.' The doctor gave a shudder, and his spoon rang outside the edge of the pink ice-cream dish.

'You just need to look in any orphanage, or even pick up a homeless kid on the corner – anything would be better than her,' said Cholyshev.

'You are wrong, Pasha. Let me explain. I am a non-practising Jew. A general practitioner, and – to be honest – not a brilliant doctor. In my life I have seen only diseases and believed only in medicine. But in my heart, Pasha, there was a gaping hole. Don't get me wrong: I love and respect my wife. But when you live a long time together and have no children, your wife stops being a wife – she becomes part of yourself. Before we took in the child I felt nothing but emptiness. The girl is the bane of my life, but also the meaning of my life – or rather, our life, Rosalia's and mine. Everything has its price, Pasha. But at least I – we – have someone to live for now. Bronka may be a tyrant, but we idolize her all the same, and are – don't laugh – terribly grateful to her.'

'But it's slavery!'

'And who said that love isn't slavery? Go away, Pasha. The girl won't leave you in peace, and you are not at all strong . . . You're probably a good engineer by now, but that is not enough. You have to have something more, that used to be considered God-given. Something more important than a profession. Something inside you, bigger than us. Go to Moscow.'

'And there I'll find this "something"? No, Aron Solomonovich, you can't run away from yourself.'

'Don't say things you don't understand. Moscow will make full use of you. It will exploit all your strengths and talents, if you have any, of course, and won't allow you to lounge about in bed or drink beer in the streets. You're just vegetating here.'

Who would stay in this hole if they had the chance to leave? thought Cholyshev. But it's hard to make the move. Otherwise I'd bugger off this minute! They're used to me at the design office. They've given me up as a lost case – 'politically unaware'. A Philistine. Not interested in anything unless it's in a skirt. He's a good enough worker, mind you. Draws quite well, and even thinks for himself. He's a specialist. That's why we keep him . . . But in Moscow I'd be new. I'd have to pretend to be ideologically sound. No, I'd rather hide here in my burrow. Here nobody knows how fed up I am with all that's happened, how I can't stand these posters and slogans, and those Party boors who snatched up all the merchants' villas. The doctor's going on like a Chekhov character – 'To Moscow! To Moscow!' – but in Moscow there is probably four times the amount of propaganda, and banners, and pretentious top brass as there is here. So I'll just die where I was born, and forget the bright lights. Anything rather than be driven to meetings and parades . . .

Doctor Tokar paid the waitress, and Pavel ordered some more beer. His colleague, with whom he had started an affair that summer, was afraid of Bronka and refused to come to the house on Police Street during daylight hours. But it was far better to wait for a woman at home. He took a container full of beer home, stripped to his underpants, stretched out on the cool floor, and picked up a book to read . . .

At last, after six, the copyist finished work. After a trip to an island, they were now returning home. It was quickly growing dark and cold.

Bronka was waiting for them not on the fence but on the ground, near some broken masonry.

'With your prostitute again, are you, Pashka?! Coo-ee, you whore!' the girl shouted, and the thirty-year-old woman convulsively pressed up against Pavel. A stone whistled past her head.

'Come on, come on, don't worry,' said Cholyshev.

'Oh-ooh!' wailed Bronka, as though she were playing at cowboys and Indians, and not torn with jealously.

'A-agh!' screamed the woman and covered her face with her hands. 'The little wretch, she got me in the eye!'

'Wait a minute, we'll get it washed. I'll skin her alive!' said Pavel in a fury.

'Yoo-hoo, skin me alive, then,' Bronka guffawed.

There was another whistle.

'Ow, my teeth, my teeth, the bitch . . .' the woman groaned, and stormed off – not towards Cholyshev's dilapidated house, but on to the street.

'Wait!' shouted Pavel. 'Don't call the police!'

The woman refused to obey.

'Chick-en! Chick-en!' shouted Bronka, roaring with laughter, but retreated to the fence.

'Right, you horrible brat, you're for it now!'

Cholyshev went up to the girl and took hold of her arm above the elbow.

'Let's go. She'll bring the militia in a minute. Wait till I open the door, and don't try to escape!'

He dragged the girl to the porch.

'Your hands are shaking,' said Bronka. He was indeed finding it difficult to get the key in the lock.

Now you'll sing a different tune. I'll manage without the militia, Cholyshev decided, and dragged Bronka over the sloping glass porch into the hourse.

'Lie down!' he ordered, pointing at the bed. Bronka did not resist, but flopped down on her stomach. Pavel took down from a hook his old school belt, which he used as strop to sharpen his razor in the mornings. Bronka wheezed away, without turning round.

'Ow, don't tickle!' she yelped, when he pulled up her dress.

'You'll see how I "tickle" you!' he said grimly, but suddenly got cold feet. Follows the fashions, does she? – he thought – can't wear ordinary ones . . .

Clasping the belt under his arm, he pulled Bronda's stylish silk drawers from her hips, and then, holding the belt by the buckle, lashed her with all his might.

'Aow!' she shrieked.

' "Aow", eh? D'you think stones don't hurt?!'

Suddenly there was a loud noise in the porch and somebody banged at the door. The copyist's voice was hoarse with excitement:

'Pavel Rodionovich, open up!' But Bronka had squirmed away from the belt and pressed up close to Cholyshev. Her face was wet. She must have been crying silently. Pavel at once lost the desire to flog her, and embraced her with remorse and pity. Here he was, thrashing her, and yet she loved him. That was why she threw stones. What kind of a brute was he!

Boots creaked and lights flashed outside the window, and then it became quiet and dark again. But with his hands – even more surely than with his eyes – Pavel realized just how young Bronka was. And after all, he had never been attracted to her. He had always rushed past hoping she would not pester him. But maybe he was pretending? What if it was just such an untouched, inexperienced girl he needed? He had never been with girls – he did not really know what they were . . .

Then he checked himself – What do I need her for? – but Bronka squeezed up to him and would not let him think. Desire had never left Cholyshev during those past years. It had perhaps become saturated with his youth, his ambition, and his unrealizable hopes. All this together, heightened by his rejection of the political reality and non-participation in it, was distilled into a craving to sink down and drown in a woman, if only for a night, if only for five minutes, and to hell with everything else . . . Leokadia, though fifteen years his senior, suited that dark purpose. So did the colleagues who came after her. So did the copyist. Now Bronka was nestling up against him, and she was youngest of them all . . .

'Push her away! Slap her face and send her packing . . . You'll ruin her *and* yourself . . .' some sad, wise voice whispered to him. But his hands, not listening, searched for Bronka.

'Pashka, Pashenka . . .' she sobbed, as though Cholyshev were lashing her again.

'Stop it. It's all right, it's all right,' he said, still trying to restrain himself. 'Run home now. The cops are gone . . .'

But Bronka did not listen. 'Pasha . . . Pashenka . . .' She was breathing heavily and ardently, like a grown woman.

'Phew, there's more to her than I thought!' was the last thing Pavel managed to think.

There was indeed a lot to Bronka, and it proved harder to turn the frantic girl out of the house than to submit to her.

Two hours later an embarrassed Cholyshev knocked at the Tokars' door and told them they could deal with him as they saw fit. He was prepared either for prison or for the register office. The doctor's wife wept and swore in Yiddish, and Aron Solomonovich shook his yellow-domed head and repeated: 'I warned you, Pasha . . . Why are you so weak? You're not strong, not strong at all . . .'

'Let him go to prison, the scoundrel! They won't accept them at the marriage bureau,' said Rosalia, in Russian now.

'Yes they will . . .' mumbled Pavel, as if he already knew that Bronka was pregnant.

Thus began a strange time in his life. Bronka – or Varvara Alekseyevna Cholyshev – stayed with Pavel for less than a month. Although he kept from his young wife the fact that she was a burden to him, she understood this almost at once.

'Being noble, are you?' she said bluntly. 'Well, you can go to hell with your nobility. I don't need it.'

Of course she doesn't need it, Cholyshev agreed silently. What a useless oaf I am.

'I suppose you think you're being kind?' Bronka shouted. 'There's not a drop of kindness in you. Kindness is what loving people have. All you've got is dullness and decency.'

It's all true, Pavel realized to his distress. I'm not kind, and I'm not noble. I'm callous. And that's putting it mildly. Why did she look to me, the poor devil? What did she find in me? Did she really hope that I would save her? Protect her from her crazy, unruly nature? Probably she was afraid of herself . . . But what kind of saviour am I? You can't save someone without love, and I can't even scrape up any pity. We're such strangers that I can't even think of anything to talk about with her. Oh . . . first I made her a woman, then I made her bitter, and now I must suffer . . .

'What on earth will become of the child?' The doctor's wife was already worried about Bronka's progeny.

'It's a nightmare!' Doctor Tokar echoed her, for by day Bronka was threatening to have an abortion, and by night she would run across the street to Koska Drozd, now a degenerate and a drunkard. The former grammar-school pupil had totally gone to seed, and worked in a scrapyard. When he was drunk he would bellow out to the whole street:

> Arse against the fence, Bronka,
> Smile, and press hard,
> Send the fence-posts flying
> Into the neighbour's yard.

'Awful!' the doctor repeated, but no longer asked Pavel to go away to Moscow. Somehow, he had grown attached to his son-in-law, although Cholyshev could already scarcely be called his son-in-law. Having registered the birth of her daughter, Masha, Bronka immediately divorced Pavel. She did not marry Drozd, however, but found a job in a hotel – coincidentally the same one in which her mother had been strangled.

And Cholyshev, unmarried again, led a very strange life, sleeping at his own place but taking his meals at the Tokars'.

Decades later Varvara Alekseyevna averred that Pavel and she had made a sort of agreement to that effect. But that was pure invention. Bronka and he never agreed about anything. It was just that Cholyshev was fond of his daughter, although it was no easy thing to get near her: granddad, grandma and the maid coddled the child like an heir to the throne. Bronka herself was very cool towards her baby.

('But you know, Pashet, that hypocritical way of spending your time suited you,' his second wife, Zhenya, observed later. 'All that enthusiasm on the streets, Five-Year Plans in four years, heroic

Arctic voyages and Polar expeditions, arrests in the night . . . and you were sitting in the cosy warmth of a Jewish home discussing loftier things with the old doctor. Wasn't that a perfectly ordinary case of running away from reality? Just as people who are psychologically unsure of themselves hide from the complexities of life in an illness. I'm terribly sorry for you, Pashet. Did you at least have a few affairs?'

'There was no time. I was bringing up a daughter,' replied Pavel angrily.

'You weren't over-successful in that, unfortunately,' Zhenya sighed, and there was no answer to that.)

Masha, to be sure, did not grow up as Cholyshev would have wished. There was too much obstinacy in her – too much of Bronka, as Cholyshev saw it. She constantly wanted to be noticed, she was impatient and intolerant – wanted everything the very moment she thought of it. Once, when she spotted a boy on a blue bicycle, she filled the whole of their privileged street with such a heart-rending wail of 'Buy me one like that! Buy me one!' that Cholyshev felt they might be arrested. (He had an abiding antipathy not only to bicycles but also to secretaries of city Party committees.)

With age, the thirst to be above everyone and ahead of everyone began to inflate Masha like an athlete or a politician. At twelve she became the president of the pupils' committee. She had Bronka's vanity. Bronka, with no education, joined the Party, and by the war was running the whole hotel.

No, my daughter doesn't take after me, thought Cholyshev; but if she had done, that would have been bad, too. You couldn't hide her in a corner, or underground, or in a den, safe, like a mouse, from social pressures. A child cannot sustain solitude. Especially not a child like that – an 'active' child, as they say nowadays. And anyway, what right would I have to condemn her to a hopeless life of disaffection?

Cholyshev's own disaffection and solitude might have lasted for ever had it not been for the war. On the fourth day, although his work as a mining engineer gave him exemption, Cholyshev looked in at the enlistment office and was instantly assigned to a construction detachment. And so the following morning in the schoolyard Doctor Tokar could proudly contemplate his son-in-law all kitted out in khaki: so this is who's going to defeat Hitler! His wife blew her nose and wept. Even Bronka tactfully patted her eyelashes with a cambric handkerchief. And only Masha was conspicuously put out because her father had been issued with a canvas belt instead of a leather one, and ankle-length boots and puttees instead of knee-length box-calf boots.

For the first six months, while retreating from the Dnieper to the Donets, Pavel unfailingly sent his regards to the Tokars in his letters to Siberia. Masha sent meagre replies: 'Mum is well, I am well. Thank you very much. Your letters are arriving. We are receiving our allowance. Regards from Mum . . .' But never a word about her grandparents . . .

Then, when Cholyshev was reregistering his remittance, he divided the six hundred roubles into four hundred and two hundred, and readdressed the two hundred to Rosalia Tokar. 'The doctor might have died, but the women are tougher . . .' he deceived himself. The doctor was thin and sinewy, not affected by diabetes or sclerosis, but Rosalia was a huge carcass of a woman.

During the war, two hundred roubles was nothing – barely enough to be able to use up one's ration cards. But now Bronka responded for some reason. She wrote that the Tokars had gone missing on the journey. She knew nothing about them, although she had made enquiries at Buguruslan, where information about evacuees was gathered. And Senior Lieutenant Cholyshev considered his old neighbours as missing persons until he landed back in his home town at the end of 1943. Neighbours who had survived told him the true story, with their eyes cast down as though they were to blame, and not the Germans. But what could unarmed women have done against the Wehrmacht? The women also deserved pity. They had all aged by about ten years.

'But where are the Tokars?' Cholyshev asked, standing in the middle of the bare yard in his now reddish and ill-fitting army coat.

'They killed the – all of *them* – in the ravine, Pashenka,' said a neighbour, the same age as Cholyshev's mother would have been.

'But Rosalia Tokar would never have made it that far,' remarked Cholyshev with a frown.

'They wheeled her in a barrow,' stammered the old woman, and Pavel did not feeling like asking any more. He left without saying goodbye, and cabled Bronka that the Tokars had been shot and that their house (it had been used as a sort of soldiers' barracks) had been burned by the Germans when they left. He did not say that the rooms had actually survived the fire and that even the simple furniture had not been touched.

Saturday was slowly wearing on. The kitchen clock cuckooed twice. But Zhenya did not look up from the typewriter, and the old man had little choice but to take the next batch of pages. He read about the poet Yuz being arrested, and about how Nadka felt sorry for him but did not go to Dzerzhinsky Street to ask about him. Mind you, what would have been the point of going, since the Ukrainian newspaper had branded him a 'Trotskyist and bourgeois nationalist'. Yudif was horrified. She took medicine and hissed: 'Should have known better than to take that kid to their bandits' parade! Now they'll send our little orphan to a home, and Nadka to some place where you can't get enough warm clothes and you don't need any graces because the ladies wear quilted jackets . . .'

But the town was soon caught up in such pandemonium that they forgot not only about Grisha and Nadka, but even about their father. The new occupant of the First Secretary's villa was arrested, and his successor, too, did not enjoy its comforts for long.

'That's what they get, the traitors!' Yudif rejoiced, and gazed at her nephew and niece ever more tenderly and sadly. It was as if she sensed that she did not have much longer to admire them. And sure enough, the following spring, having caught cold, Yudif advised Nadka to get a job at a clothes factory, and then departed to a better world, in the cemetery behind the red brick wall, close to the post marking where Mother's urn was interred.

. . . Then the memoirs introduced Mother's Moscow friend, Aunt Susanna, with whom Grisha stayed during the summer holidays, in the same dark, narrow room where his mother Dora had prematurely passed away. Moscow overwhelmed the boy. But one day Stalin's youthful favourite tumbled in to see Aunt Susanna. He was a bit tipsy, and disheartened by the presence of the young lad. Learning that this was Dora's son, the handsome fellow muttered gloomily, 'The image of his mother,' and ruffled the boy's hair.

He'll probably betray me too, like Uncle August, thought Grishna warily, and reluctantly answered his questions: 'Yes, I work hard at school. Yes, I write poems.'

Throughout this, the boy noticed that Aunt Susanna's excited eyes never wavered from the guest.

Sobering up, the grey-haired man asked Grisha to recite something he had written. He read a poem about a train-driver getting drunk and causing a whole train full of Red Army soldiers to leave the rails. The guest, scowling, explained to Aunt Susanna that the poem was not merely decadent, but even, so to speak, slanderous. Of course, during the Civil War the soldiers of the Red Army did on occasion have a drink of vodka – he himself as a boy partisan sometimes had a 'warmer-upper'. But one had to sift the typical from the accidental, as it were, and drunkenness – especially on the railways – was certainly not a typical phenomenon. It wasn't right to defame our railwaymen. If the driver were transporting Red Army reinforcements, he would not drink under any circumstances. And if he was a counter-revolutionary he would have jumped out before they reached the bend, to save his own skin, so to speak, and drinking wouldn't have come into it.

'Read something based on fact,' he went on in a milder tone. 'About school, for instance. Or about your sister. What is Nadya up to, by the way? Ah-ha, you see, your sister is the heroic working class. Or what about your girlfriend? Don't tell me you haven't written a poem about her?'

'I haven't,' Grisha blushed, and looked anxiously at Aunt Susanna to whom only a few days before he had read two verses about Masha Cholyshev. But Aunt Susanna, completely forgetting about the heroine of Grisha's heart, voiced agreement with the handsome grey guest: of course, of course, one must write about life and only about what one had experienced oneself . . .

The boy was mortally offended. And although in Moscow there was the metro, museums, the Agricultural Exhibition, and no problems with food, he longed to return to his sister, and left before the end of the holidays. But in the clay-walled house he discovered a well-built young student of the Transport College who bore a vague resemblance to the grey-haired man in Moscow. He lounged about on Yudif's bed, lazily flicking through *Twenty Years On*, while Nadka, unafraid of the revenue inspector, treadled away at the sewing machine, even making skirts and dresses. At nights the rattling of the machine gave way to a no less desperate rattling of Yudif's bed. But the student did not notice Grisha, as though he were an inanimate object that one bumped against in the dark when hurrying to answer nature's call.

But in the middle of autumn the transport student started spending the night more and more often at the hostel, and then suddenly joined a ski battalion and left for the Karelian isthmus. Nadka sobbed her heart out, and suffered from some prolonged and serious illness, and the Tokars were unexpectedly visited by Varvara Alekseyevna, Masha's mother. She was surprised by how uncomfortable, cold and hungry they were in the ramshackle house. The brother and sister ate bread and vegetable-marrow puree, and jacket potatoes.

But Grisha did not care about his conditions. He was saddened by his poetry, and by Nadka. She started coming home drunk, and it was impossible even to elicit from her whether she was working or on sick leave again. Increasingly, Grisha would meet his sister near the Astoria hotel, which Masha's mother ran. The hotel was just opposite the Pioneers' (formerly the governor's) Palace, where Grisha attended the literature club. Those days were long past when his sister would whisper: 'Grishka, we are better off than others.'

Now she flew off the handle at the slightest thing. Her face looked pinched. She had black bags under her eyes, and Varvara Alekseyevna, coming into the house once, burst out laughing: 'Rebecca! What a beautiful Rebecca!'

'She's called Nadya,' said her brother angrily.

'I know, I know. What I'm saying is she's the Rebecca type.'

At the literature club the children mocked Grisha: 'Give up poetry. You rhyme "boots" and "knee-boots".'

Grisha flew out of the Palace as though catapulted, and, as luck would have it, Masha Cholyshev came riding towards him on her blue bicycle, smiling superciliously. He felt like dying. The only consolation was Aunt Susanna's promise to have him in Moscow again for the summer.

Eventually a third-class ticket was bought, but the day before he was to depart Molotov announced the outbreak of war. There were air-raids, people were digging slit-trenches everywhere, and the usual nickname of 'Jewboy' began to sound like a grim threat. For that reason Nadka, as though awakening from a drunken sleep, stopped painting her lips and drinking wine, and started stitching sacks together. For it was precisely sacks they needed, with straps, rather than suitcases. Even the sewing machine, minus its stand, Nadka packed away in a specially-made rucksack. With the machine they would not starve. All they had to do was to find a smallish town, somewhere beyond the Urals.

Nadka made up with her brother again, and now if she went to see Masha's mother it was for a different reason – to beg her to take them with her . . .

And so they ended up in a heated goods van! The station was jammed with wagons of all colours and sizes. An idea for a poem formed in Grisha's mind, comparing the couplers with gypsies. He was terribly thirsty, but Masha's mother would not allow him to jump out of the van.

'When the train starts moving it will be cooler,' Nadka reassured her brother.

Makeshift bunks had been erected in the car, and Masha Cholyshev clambered up to the top one. Her plaits lay across a pink pillow-slip. All the evacuees here were from the city council and municipal departments. Grisha and his sister, allowed on out of charity, squatted by the door on their sacks.

'Gri-isha-a!' called Masha, stretching her lips. 'Gri-i-isha!'

Underneath, just below Masha, sat Varvara Alekseyevna. She was exhausted from running backwards and forwards between the Pullman car, where the top brass were, and the goods van, putting things in order and distributing food. In the morning everyone apart from the Tokar children had been given bread, butter, and even salami which had long since disappeared from the shops. But in this heat Grisha wanted only to drink, not eat.

'Gri-i-sha-a!' Masha teased, and Grisha turned away. Now he was facing an engine pipe, from which mouthfuls of water were dripping.

Suddenly a voice was heard calling from the back of the train: 'Bronka! Bronechka! Masha!' Varvara Alekseyevna shuddered and, looking evilly at Nadka and Grisha, pressed a finger to her lips, as if to say: you say a word and I'll throw you off this train. And on the upper bunk little Masha covered her face with the pillow.

Outside, stumbling along the railway tracks, were the stooping Doctor Tokar and his enormous wife, looking as though she were pumped full of water. The doctor was carrying a shabby medical travelling bag, his wife a handbag. With the old woman clinging to her husband's arm, they were weaving their way between the trains – he an old Don Quixote, she a legless Sancho Panza.

'Bronya! Bronechka! Masherochka!' Their voices carried to the goods van.

Little Masha pressed up against the side of the car.

'Nadya, come and shield me,' whispered Varvara Alekseyevna, and Nadya, sobbing, moved in front of her.

'And you get away from the door,' she hissed to Grisha, but the boy stared at the approaching old people as though bewitched.

'You there, my boy, you must be Tokar?' said the doctor joyfully, as though Grisha was his grandson, and not merely his namesake.

'Are you Tokar, boy?' repeated his wife, and Grisha merely nodded, as if his lips were sealed with wax.

'Aron, you're right! It's Tokar! He'll tell us where Bronka is.'

But Grisha could not reply: 'She is here,' because he had already visualized Varvara Alekseyevna hurling the rucksacks out on to the coal-covered ground, and pushing Nadka and himself out after them. Instead the boy found himself whispering, like an incantation: 'Help me, somebody! Somebody help . . .'

And the train did indeed give a jolt, the wheels clattered over the joints in the rails, the goods van jerked, and the old Tokars stood paralysed with horror, looking at the boy in silent reproach.

'So that's how it was!' Old Cholyshev glowered at his wife. Why did she push this manuscript on me? She could have waited until Varvara Alekseyevna was dead. It's too late to settle accounts with a sentenced person. And Masha . . .? Why, Masha was just a child. It's cruel to shove me into all this! What can I change now? And anyway, can Grishka be believed?

The old man glared at his wife like a hunted animal, but she was absorbed in her work. The telephone rang. Cholyshev counted the rings and listened to see whether Zhenya slowed down her typing speed. At the eleventh ring she gave in and picked up the receiver. 'Yes . . .'

'Have you gone deaf, or is a night's sleep not enough for you?!'

It seemed to the old man as if his daughter's voice was coming not from the black plastic but from Zhenya's sleeve.

'It's for you . . .'

Zhenya laid the receiver on the day-bed.

'Why don't you answer the phone?' shouted Masha. 'Mum's died!'

'I'm sorry, dear. I'll be right there . . . I'm sorry . . .'

Cholyshev wanted to add something, but hesitated and blushed, watching Zhenya with displeasure. She was typing. Then the line went dead, and the old man felt easier.

'I'm going. Varvara Alekseyevna is dead,' he uttered drily.

'Oh Lord, Pashet . . .'

Zhenya stood before him no longer looking youthful, but frightened, and fifty-three.

'Pashet, let's go together . . .'

'Stay here.'

Or should he take her, so she would not be typing? It seemed to the old man that Zhenya should now destroy Grishka's memoirs. But there was a sheet of paper in the typewriter, the notebook was lying open, and a fresh pile of pages was neatly piled up on the bureau.

'You stay here. I'll go . . .' He looked at his wife and was taken aback by how she had aged. 'It's easier alone,' he added with pity in his voice, and Zhenya began to grow youthful again as though going back in the train to the Siberia of 1945.

'Poor Pashet,' she said, hugging him. Once again she was that dear woman he knew from the half-awake hours of morning, and nighttime, and Saturdays and Sundays and holidays – of any time of day, when he gazed at her with eyes full of love, not noticing the years or wrinkles, or anything except her dear face, which grew old only when they argued, when his vision became harsh and his memory poor.

'Wait here. I'll be back soon. It's not worth your going there today. She . . .' the old man intentionally did not say his daughter's name – ' is upset.'

But when he got outside, Cholyshev realized that he did not want to see either Bronka or Masha.

'It would have been better if I'd been killed in the war,' he said to himself with annoyance. But the engineers suffered few casualties, and Cholyshev was not even scratched. For the first time he was lucky. Even the fact that their unit was not moved into Yugoslavia showed the hand of fortune. For Klim was living in Yugoslavia; presumably he was alive, at least, since he could scarcely have been over sixty at that time. But Captain Cholyshev had declared in dozens of questionnaires: 'I have no relations abroad.' Consequently, Klim did not exist.

And so Europe, instead of complications with the personnel department, promised an almost idyllic life and abundant pleasures.

But suddenly in March a letter arrived from Masha.

Dad, I haven't written for a long time – I didn't want to upset you. There wasn't much you could do from so far away. . . But my patience has run out. Mum is carrying on in such a way that at this rate we'll soon end up in clink. She's got a fancy-man. He keeps thrusting himself upon me, but he's as old as the hills – an old partisan. . . Dad, take me away from here. If you've got a sweetheart, it doesn't matter. I'm broad-minded. We'll get on all right.

> With much love,
> Masha

Cholyshev's first thought was to ask for leave.

'We're not Germans. We're not entitled to that kind of leave,' scowled the unit commander, who had already twice taken leave to see his 'main' wife in Gorky, and also had a short-term one in the army. Exhausted by bigamy, alcohol, cards and a fear of all kinds of alerts, the lieutenant-colonel also did not want to let Masha come and stay with the unit.

'For goodness' sake, Cholyshev! She'll be gang-banged before she can sneeze. The lads are desperate. You say your daughter's at school? Fine: leave her there.'

However, Captain Cholyshev dug his heels in, and the lieutenant-colonel, not wishing to quarrel with an officer who did the work of four, grudgingly signed a recommendation. The documents were sent out, but Masha did not reply.

The old man chose the most roundabout route: first he took a trolleybus, then transferred to a bus, then got on another trolleybus, but his sense of hurt still did not subside. He was as unprepared as ever for Bronka's death. Death with a capital D, as Klim used to say. Klim used to write the whole word DEATH in capitals, and underline it.

Entering at last an old and dismal Moscow courtyard, Cholyshev climbed the decrepit back staircase to the first floor and saw a door standing open. That meant the men from the mortuary hadn't been yet, and all his detours had been in vain. . . He pushed open the door and found himself in the cramped room that served as entrance-hall and kitchen. His son-in-law was writing something at the table. When he saw Cholyshev he jumped up, still slim and robust, and cried out with indecorous joy: 'Masha, Pashet's here!'

'Don't bawl,' tutted his wife, coming out of the living-room, and the old man caught sight of a bed, with something covered in a threadbare sheet, between the wall and a yellow screen.

No amount of shouting will wake her up now, he thought, still not wishing to go near the body.

'You've been long enough about it. I'm surprised you didn't get dusty,' said Marsha sarcastically, evidently divining her father's feelings.

'It's impossible to find a taxi on Saturdays,' said Grisha, trying to protect his father-in-law.

'Grishka and I are absolutely washed out,' Masha yawned. 'If Mother had been taken away, you'd never have woken us up.'

'Let's go and see her . . .' mumbled the old man, overcoming himself, and made to embrace his daughter.

'I'm tired,' Masha moved away and went into the room first.

Cholyshev sank down on to a chair, glad of the screen for the respite it granted.

'That's the way of it, Pashet,' sighed his son-in-law, sitting down at the other side of the dining table. It was a large room – about thirty square metres. And it had an unlived-in feel about it, being crammed full of heterogeneous furniture that could almost have been requisitioned: a polished writing desk, an old oak sideboard, a scruffy veneered wardrobe, a red child's divan, and now the screen as well. And yet, it was not just lived-in; people died here too.

'Dad, come here,' called Masha from behind the screen, but just at that moment the doorbell rang twice and Grishka cried 'At last!' and ran to the door. But instead of the undertaker it was a young man with a musketeer beard and curling chestnut-coloured locks who came in. The old man remembered that he had met him briefly once before at his daughter's place, and had instantly written him off as one of her lovers.

'Good afternoon, Pavel Rodionovich,' said the new arrival, breaking into a smile as though he were making a present of himself rather than just saying hello. 'Hello, old man!' he said as he embraced Griskha. 'Varvara Alekseyevna . . .?' He sighed meaningfully. 'Too bad, too bad . . .'

'She's dead . . .' said Masha tearfully and laid her head on the young man's shoulder.

'Let me go to her and pray. It's all right, Mariushka, I'll go alone . . .' And, gently pushing Masha aside, the bearded guest disappeared behind the screen.

He's trying, thought Cholyshev. He's trying, though he's not a priest . . .

'Her face is nice . . . Radiant . . .' said the guest, returning. He rubbed his palms with pleasure, as though he had just eaten something, and hugged Masha.

'Wash your hands!' exclaimed the old man.

'Are you afraid of the dead?' smiled the hairy young man. 'There's no need to fear them, Pavel Rodionovich. They have already departed.'

'How come she's got a "radiant" face if "they have already departed"?' Cholyshev felt like asking, but restrained himself. It wasn't the dead in general he was afraid of, just Bronka. He still did not love her, just as when she was alive.

No, he's no priest, Cholyshev thought, looking at the young man. He's an amateur. Appointed himself priest. But the priesthood isn't just a profession or a job – in Russia it's destiny. I'd swear there was more faith in Klim's decision to unfrock himself than in this fop's attitude . . .

The guest lit up a long cigarette. In this, too, he differed from Cholyshev's uncle. Klim used to roll his own with home-grown tobacco. What does a graveyard pope earn? This bearded fellow was bang up to date, in American jeans and a suede jacket.

The morgue certainly isn't hurrying . . . The old man remembered about the undertakers. If only they would arrive before Masha calls me behind the screen . . .

Meanwhile the shaggy-haired guest, lolling in a chair and already forgetful of the newly-deceased, launched an attack on the Pope and Catholicism. It was a satanic faith, he claimed, which denied the feelings of the people and enticed only the proud . . . Grishka Tokarev listened intently, but Masha went back to her mother.

Now she'll go and call me, thought old Cholyshev. 'Love your enemies . . .' That's an old story . . . But Bronka I cannot . . .

And, looking for a straw to grasp at on this side of the screen, he interrupted the guest: 'Orthodoxy, young man, did not protect us from the Mongols. Who knows, perhaps Catholicism would have done. You say it's against the people? But the people followed it, and the Catholics had power. When the Mongol Horde poured into Russia and our popes did nothing to help the princes stand up to it, in the West the priests were gathering the loafers to go and win back the Holy Sepulchre – and they obeyed like children! And if the princes had fought off the Tatars, Russia wouldn't have been lumbered with the Asiatic yoke for seven whole centuries. People would have set up Habeas Corpus, instead of village communes and bloody communal living.'

'Catholicism in Russia?! That's all we needed!' said Masha, looking out from behind the screen. 'Mother is dead, and you are afraid to go near her and blabber on about God knows what! Even at a time like this you want to get at her – as if to say: you chose the wrong religion! Or do you think everybody should pray in his own corner? Me in the chapel like my grandmother, Grishka in the synagogue. What would he want in a synagogue? He's Russian. He's better than all of you! It was he, not you, who opened my eyes . . .' Masha suddenly turned on the bearded guest.

'What is it, Masha? Am I arguing?' said the latter, blushing, and old Cholyshev was confirmed in his suspicions.

'Grishka is the best of the lot of you . . .' wept Masha and went behind the screen again. But when she sat down on the narrow bed at her mother's feet, Masha realized that her shouting was overdone. She was not *so* saddened by Varvara Alekseyevna's death. She had never loved her mother. She had pitied her, yes, but even that did not last long.

It was true that at first Varvara Alekseyevna had been a puzzle to the little girl. Beautiful and majestic, a real lady, she had for some reason preferred Kostya the rag-and-bone man to her engineer husband. The women in the yard explained that it was Love! But that magical word simply did not tie in with that vodka-bloated idler. Masha knew that her mother was abandoned as a child, and that such people have peculiar traits. They have no great liking for ordinary people and are drawn towards outcasts. Was that not why Mother took care of Grishka Tokar's good-for-nothing sister?

When the war broke out, Mother lost her head entirely. Kostya Drozd did not want to be evacuated, and she herself almost stayed behind. But then she changed her mind, and took with her in the goods van not her foster parents, but the other Tokars.

'The train isn't elastic-sided,' she explained to Masha. 'It's a case of either – or . . . Who has most future for the motherland? Young people, full of strength, or people with one foot in the grave? Do you understand? In that case stop bleating about it. Neither one pair nor the other are my relations, and I'm acting fairly.'

In evacuation Masha shot up and matured, and at fourteen she already looked of age. She could turn men's heads. Just by narrowing her light-green eyes she deprived her geography teacher, discharged with shell-shock, of speech for half a lesson. The riff-raff that hung around the dance halls and the cinema considered Masha an 'easy lay'. And only her mother's lover, a former Red partisan and now her boss, Mikhail Stepanich, paid no attention to her. It was with him that the Cholyshevs lived. The Red partisan was considered to have shown great conscientiousness by sharing his living space. Both his sons were at the front, and his wife had gone to visit relatives just before the war and been stranded in occupied territory. Mikhail Stepanich now locked himself up with Masha's mother in their two adjoining rooms, leaving Masha the spacious kitchen.

When it came down to it, why should Masha have bothered about her mother's admirer? There was no need even to think about him. Indeed, she did not think about him. What was the head of a Workers' Supplies Board to her? She was better fed and clothed than many Siberians. But she was furious with her mother. Why did she move in with the Red partisan? She didn't love him in the slightest. She was just trying to get up among the bosses herself, so that she too would have secretaries sitting outside her office, and people making appointments to see her a whole week in advance. And when she felt like it, she would hand out a kilo of millet here, and a pair of felt boots there, and when she felt bloody-minded, she would refuse. Mother enjoyed ordering about the needy and the unfortunate.

And you know, if you looked closely, Varvara Alekseyevna wasn't even all that beautiful. Masha's looks were by no means inferior. She was taller and had a better figure, and her eyes were lighter. Her mother's eyes were dark with worry because she was constantly striving for advantage. Masha could avenge herself without ceremony: she could prove without bias that her mother was a nasty bit of work. Why did she leave her husband? Why did she abandon Grandma and Granddad to the

Germans? Let her pay for it all . . .

And so Masha gradually began to compete with her mother. She might guffaw loudly at one of her lover's stupid jokes, or else stare rapturously at him, as if he wasn't a *former* partisan but a modern one, young and dashing. Her efforts were not in vain. Mikhail Stepanich picked up the scent and went on the alert, and soon you couldn't tell who was hunting whom.

This was where she should have broken off. She had achieved her aim. But Masha got carried away, and the test of her youthful charms led her too far. Once, her mother's fancy-man went mad and sat her on his knee. Masha tore herself away from him, but throughout the next week she waited fearfully and with sinking heart for the Red partisan to pounce on her again.

All this went on in silence. Masha now hated her mother. Sometimes she imagined that her mother knew about everything but looked through her fingers at it, as if to say: you fool, fancy trying to measure your strength with me! So what if Mikhail Stepanich touches you a bit – that's harmless enough . . .

In fact Varvara Alekseyevna was quite in the dark about it all. Her paramour slipped home during the day. Parking his car near some office, the head of the Workers' Supplies Board trotted across the yard and puffed up the stairs to his flat. Masha had given up school long ago. Now she heard his heavy, irresolute steps on the stairs. The key turned in the lock. Masha stood in the kitchen, repeating in a whisper: 'Filthy bastard, filthy bastard . . .'

She herself had no intention of rushing out to him, and Mikhail Stepanich went through to the adjoining rooms, and spent time moving things about, although he had only minutes to spare.

Masha whispered more and more impatiently, 'Filthy bastard . . .' But the partisan behaved as though the flat was empty. Finally he went back into the hall and turned the key in the lock. Masha pressed her burning forehead against the cold metal of the water-tap. Well, who was hunting whom . . .?

And then the partisan pushed open the kitchen door . . .

'What jolly games we played . . .' thought Masha with a shudder. It seemed as if she had been sitting an eternity with her dead mother. On the other side of the screen the argument was just warming up.

'Of course, one can blame the Orthodox Church for not uniting the princes to repulse the Tatar invasion,' Masha's friend was saying. 'But you will agree, Pavel Rodionovich, that that is a pragmatic view, and therefore totally alien to the Russian mind. The Mongols were Russia's Golgotha. They were sent down upon Russia in atonement for her sins. Any other view is not merely blasphemous, but absurd. There were fewer Mongols than Russians, and if it hadn't been preordained, the Russians would have beaten the Asiatics back.'

'Like the Magyars and Czechs?' asked Cholyshev.

'More or less . . . But Russia had a different path open to it. And the Czechs and Hungarians, having driven back the Mongols, stagnated in their bourgeois-gluttonous semi-sinfulness.'

'And that's why we later flattened them with tanks, is it?'

'We're speaking about something different,' frowned the guest.

'Dad, stop blaspheming!' shouted Masha from behind the screen, and the old man felt uncomfortable.

Only six months before, Masha had published an article in the journal *Science and Religion*, and however much her father had tried to persuade her that it was a dishonourable thing to do, she had ignored his admonitions: religion, she said, was just a deception that softened the brain. One need have no qualms, therefore, about refuting the lie of the Church. And anyway, what else could one write honestly about these days? 'You're obsessed with the Church! What have you got against it?' Cholyshev had sighed at the time, and reminded her of a joke: 'A drunk man is looking under a street-light for a rouble. "Where did you drop it?" asks a passer-by. "Under the hedge." "Why are you looking here, then?" "Because it's light here!" That's what you're all like,' the old man had added. 'You don't write about real issues, but about what is permitted. And you're supposed to be the most honest section . . .'

That was how things stood only half a year ago. And now his daughter's long-haired friend was babbling: 'It was Russia's good fortune that Prince Vladimir adopted Orthodoxy . . .'*

And old Cholyshev thought angrily: it would be better if she just slept with him, without the religious disputes . . . But Masha could evidently no longer exist without disputes.

'Vladimir didn't have much choice,' said Cholyshev aloud. 'It was all predetermined, only not by Heaven but by perfectly lowly circumstances.'

'Which do you mean, Pashet?' asked his son-in-law.

'Ge-og-ra-phy. The Dnieper flowed from north to south, that is, from Scandinavia to Greece. The traders took down goods to sell, and brought back the Church. Where else could they go, except Byzantium? There aren't any rivers leading to the Catholics. To the west there are forests, and the Carpathians. Even the Tatars didn't get through.'

'Geographically speaking, you may be right,' conceded the guest. 'But then geography is also preordained . . . Pavel Rodionovich, why do you depict the Russian fate so indifferently, without a trace of sorrow? Are we in your opinion a people with no alternative?'

'Not at all. But when you're late, there's no time to choose a path. Now if the Lord had deigned to situate Russia in the Aegean Sea or the Adriatic, things might have turned out better. But he stuck it in the middle of the snows and the forests, where the only routes were by water. And that water flowed to Byzantium. And ever since then, however much we try to hack our way through, we'll never reach Europe. It's quieter and more comfortable facing east. No need to be ashamed of our backwardness in front of the Mongolians and Chinese.'

'You have a strange kind of patriotism. Pavel Rodionovich, forgive me, but it seems to me there's something weighing on your mind . . . If you wish, I'll come to your flat and chat about it. Perhaps I can help.'

*Vladimir, Prince of Kievan Rus, adopted Christianity in the year 988. [Tr.]

He's speaking to me like a psychiatrist, thought Cholyshev with a smirk, but replied: 'It's always a pleasure. But we can talk in front of the others.'

'Naturally, Mariushka and Grishka are no hindrance. But you're upset today. Death has frightened you.'

'It's closer to me.'

'No one knows when it will take him. So don't be afraid of death or of the dead.'

What's this greenhorn saying! – thought Cholyshev angrily. 'Don't be afraid of the dead!!' Young Pashka Cholyshev was not afraid of them once. There was that week in the mortuary. But his fear was suppressed by sin. 'But if sin exists, then God must exist,' the old man said to himself, and the unexpectedness of this conclusion confused him.

The doorbell gave a long, urgent buzz that left no doubt: they had come for the body. However, a hefty fair-haired fellow in a railway uniform burst into the room. Even Masha, who was tall, came up only to his shoulder. For a couple of minutes she embraced the good-looking newcomer and wept, and then the railwayman stretched out his hand to the long-haired guest and named himself: 'Viktor Cholyshev.'

The long-haired man gave Pavel a puzzled look, wondering how he could have produced such a Viking.

'Just a namesake,' said the old man with a grin.

'Dad, stop playing the clown!' Masha let fly at him.

'So, I'm your namesake,' said the Viking with a frown. 'Does that bother you?'

'What are you saying? Viktor!' The long-haired fellow omitted Viktor's patronymic, suspecting some sort of family secret.

'We didn't expect you so soon,' said Masha. 'Did they put a message through to you?'

'Yes. We were supposed to be unloading this morning, but the cold store was closed. So I came here straight away.'

'Viktor transports meat,' said Grishka Tokarev.

'Feeding the capital?' asked the bearded chap gently.

'That's right.'

'Not forgetting himself . . .' said the old man mockingly.

'Dad, I'll throw you out!' Masha threatened.

'Really, Pashet, what's this all about?' said his son-in-law, blushing.

'Let him blather . . . Am I starving?' The railwayman poured scorn on the old man. 'Do I need meat? Am I in the north? Just recently we were unloading at the White Sea – that was a real laugh. The whole station came out to watch. I was tormenting this grumpy old bloke. "What are you staring at?" I asked. "Never seen frozen meat before?" And he chirps back: "Once upon a time I did, but not any more. What lucky folks are you taking it to?" "This consignment," I says, "is for the fur farms. Polar foxes can't eat concentrated millet, can they?" Well, he starts screaming at me: "You don't feed people, you bastards, and the bloody animals get it!" So I grabs him by the jacket and says: "What kind of fur have you got, mister?" Ha-ha!!' The Viking burst out laughing.

And I'm supposed to listen to this creep's fairy-tales! thought the old man. 'I'm going,' he said, and got up. 'Maybe the undertakers won't come at all . . .'

'And was it them you came to see?' Masha flared up.

Pavel turned red with shame, but, afraid to change his mind, hobbled towards the door.

'Sit down! Dad, sit down at once! So that's it! Well, I'll make you pay for this. One day you'll lie at my feet!' shouted Masha.

'Masha! Pashet!' Grishka ran out to the kitchen, but the old man was already going down the back stairs.

'Where do you think you're going, you old crank?' said Tokarev, and went back into the room. Masha was sobbing and hugging the railwayman again. Tokarev felt bored and wished they would hurry up and take away his mother-in-law, so that he could absent himself with a clear conscience.

Masha was also eager to find some distraction. But where could she go? – apart from into the past . . .

In the last winter of the war, not only the senior pupils from the boys' school were in love with her, but even the walking wounded from the hospitals. Even 'Valyaba the Boxer', the twenty-year-old ringleader of the town's ruffians (freed from service for some unknown reason) called Masha a 'star of fortune'.

Once at the Miners' Club Masha bumped into Grishka Tokar, whom she had not seen for three years. Nadka occasionally visited Varvara Alekseyevna, but Grishka avoided the Cholyshevs. Apparently he could not forgive them for deserting the old folk. And yet, if they had not deserted them Grishka would not have been living in this Siberian town and would not have been waltzing now with a big bespectacled woman. She was wearing a kerchief, padded jacket, quilted trousers, and felt boots, and looked like a watchwoman or casual worker. But Masha guessed that she was the Tokars' lodger – recently freed from a labour camp.

It was clear that Grishka would not of his own accord ask Masha to dance. But for some reason she felt like gliding over the dance floor with him in this stuffy, damp barrack. Grisha had changed greatly – he was taller and, not exactly grown-up, but good-looking in a sad sort of way, quite unlike Boxer and his cronies, or that bull, the Red partisan! Why was she with them instead of Grisha? With Grisha everything would be different, and Masha herself would become different from what she was now: breezy and coarse and hateful to herself. There was something terribly unprotected about Grishka that made one feel sorry for him. He was so thin and frail – certainly not made for Siberian life. Unabashed, however, he was squeezing this beggar-woman to him and was not remotely ashamed of her.

Of course, honest poverty and all that . . . grinned Masha, and suddenly imagined how his four-eyed partner would funk when she, Masha, went up to Grisha and embraced him in front of everyone.

'I used to be friendly with that boy,' she said to Boxer, at once fancying that she really had been.

'He's a weakling,' grunted Valyaba. 'I'll smash his snotty nose.'

'Just you try!'

'Try what?!'

But Masha had made up her mind. And scarcely had the one-armed master of ceremonies announced, 'Last dance – a waltz. Ladies' choice!' when she ran over to Grishka and looked defiantly at his bespectacled partner. The latter looked down gloomily, as though understanding that the last waltz would not end peacefully. And to be sure, Valyaba and his gang, swaying menacingly, had already crept out of the hall into the vestibule.

'Well, Grishka,' Masha almost asked, 'how are your purity and honesty doing?' She was angry that he had turned shy and was dancing woodenly, even treading on her pumps. And yet he had just been whirling round his beggar-woman quite stylishly. Proud, but a bit of a coward – thought Masha. Surely I can rouse him . . .

Suddenly, disregarding the music, Masha dragged Grishka over to the corner where her army sheepskin coat was draped over the back of a chair, and her tall, leather-trimmed white felt boots were standing.

'Help me!' She held out a boot to Grisha. 'It's a tight fit.'

Despite the simplicity of wartime manners, Grishka blushed, and his hands shook. But Masha beamed. Now both the woman in spectacles and Valyaba and Co. could see: Grishka wasn't shaking from fear, but because Masha was so beautiful.

And I *am* beautiful, she thought. How can you compare me with their lodger?! I just hope Grishka doesn't get put to shame out in the vestibule. So long as he can hold out for half a minute, and then I'll rescue him. When I give Valyaba the word he'll lay off. He's like a lamb with me . . .

With the hiss of needle on paper label, the waltz ended, and the watchwoman and disabled MC started chasing the dancers out of the warm hall into the freezing night, where there was nothing except the empty fields and the eerie creak of the snow. The woman with the glasses was waiting at the door with a tired and despondent expression, and Grishka mumbled: 'Let me introduce you. Zheka, this is Masha Cholyshev . . .'

Masha barely nodded in response. In her lambskin hat and sheepskin coat, tied with a leather belt, she imagined herself a real pin-up girl, and it felt awkward just to stand beside this scarecrow in quilted trousers.

'Let's go out and have a little chat . . .' yawned the Boxer, lazily taking hold of Grishka's collar.

He'll tear it! thought Masha with alarm, at first feeling sorry not for Grishka but for his threadbare autumn coat.

'Valka, don't you dare!' she shouted, not at all threateningly. Boxer nodded silently to his henchmen and they slowly, as though also reluctantly, started twisting Masha's arms.

'Grishka! Don't worry! He's just trying to scare you! It'll be all right!' Masha shouted breathlessly, hoping that some brave person would run to their aid.

'What're you waiting for? Move!' Boxer said indifferently, as if he had not heard his 'star of fortune' shouting, and gave Grishka a shove, but suddenly he found himself reeling towards the wall.

'You lay one finger on him . . .' said the woman with glasses in a lifeless voice, and stepped forward to shield Grishka.

'Hello, we've got an edgy one here, have we?' said Valyaba. 'Fancy a look round Heaven, eh? Easy! I can arrange it. Just show me where to stick this in . . . Get that jacket off – shame to spoil the padding!'

A sheath-knife, more like a scalpel than a gangster's knife, flashed in his hand. Masha shuddered, but the woman did not even blink.

'You louse!' she said, as though intentionally trying to goad him.

'What did you say, you whore!' screamed Valyaba, and Masha realized that he was not quite himself. He couldn't fight with a knife in his hand: he didn't have the guts for murder.

'Skunk . . . Fairy . . .' the woman continued, and suddenly launched into such a long, intricate and filthy oath that Valyaba's cronies let out a guffaw, and Grishka was struck dumb. The woman screwed up her face in disgust and looked at Valyaba as though he really was a fresh heap of shit.

Masha screwed her eyes: he'll slash her. She's a psychopath – she's asking for it . . . She's come out from there – doesn't give a damn about herself. She just wants to put me to shame, and show Grishka who she is and who I am . . . Valka's going to stab her . . . Suddenly Masha had a brainwave.

'Valka!' she shouted, with a surge of hope. 'Are you blind? Don't you see? She's one of us – from the camps . . .'

'Why the fuck didn't you say so?' said Boxer with delight. 'How was I to know – with her all wrapped up like a nun, and a mug like that . . . And pansy-boy here's the same . . . OK, beat it . . .' He waved his knife at them as he led away his gang of thugs and his 'star of fortune'.

An hour later, after rubbing Valyaba's sticky kisses from her cheeks with a piece of ice, Masha stormed home and in a flood of tears started attacking her mother and her partisan. They blinked dumbly as Masha shouted that 'this reptile, this filthy bastard' kept pawing at her every day, and that her mother saw nothing, or pretended not to so that the filthy reptile bastard wouldn't leave her.

Finally Masha locked herself up in the kitchen. Muffled screams drifted through to her from the room across the passage. But Masha was not interested in how Varvara Alekseyevna would deal with the Red partisan. Even the vague suspicion that her mother was pregnant did not touch the girl. Masha had decided to go to her father.

Sunday morning was bluish like frozen milk. The snow squeaked happily, as though glad that Masha was leaving her pretty footprints in it as a memory. At the post office they gave her a piece of wrapping paper to write on. The pen-nib kept sticking on the hairs and spattering the pale, unscrupulously diluted ink. But today it did not annoy her.

Short and precise, Masha said to herself. So he doesn't think about it, and sends the documents straight away.

She folded the letter into a triangle and dropped it into the pillar-box. The previous day's events suddenly seemed distant, and Masha strolled home calmly, prepared to be sworn at, have pots thrown at her, or even be beaten.

But they greeted her amazingly peacefully. Mother and her lover feigned smiles. A table had been carried through from the kitchen to the main room and covered with a cloth, and behind the plates of steaming and cold hors d'oeuvres, behind the decanters and bottles, Masha discerned a handsome grey-haired man with a young, almost boyish face. He got to his feet, and Masha was quite taken aback by how slim and well-built he was. Just like Grishka. But broader in the shoulders, and his suit was stupendous, as was the bluish tint of his shirt. Masha blinked as though trying to wake up. But the weak February sun cast an even light into the room. The table was creaking under all the food, and the handsome grey-haired man, walking round the mountains of food and drink, affectionately pressed Masha's head to his grey, Moscow-tailored – or possibly even imported – jacket.

If I hadn't acted so hastily then, Zhenya wouldn't be my step-mother now, Masha regretted in later years.

But that February afternoon she had no thoughts for Zhenya Knysh. The room seemed to slope like a ship's deck and Masha kept sliding towards the handsome guest. What's wrong with me? – she thought joyfully, recalling without any fear her troubles and misfortunes. Ah, yes, Mum and her dirty reptile . . . So what? What difference do they make, when this man is looking at me? He's looking at me, smiling, and understands everything. He's already guessed what's wrong with me – and since he has guessed that, he will save me. A man like that is bound to save me! He will take me away. He can do anything. I heard about him even before the war. I would never have believed that we would sit together like this. I shouldn't have written to Father. Still, the letter could go missing. And in any case, Father won't send for me; he's so ineffectual . . . But the Muscovite is very good-looking. If I believed in God I would think He wanted to save me! Or ruin me! But what's the difference? It's all the same whether I'm saved or ruined, so long as I am with this man. I'm somehow pulled towards him, but I can't cling to him. But I don't even want to cling to someone. I just want to be with him . . .

Then the guest got up to leave, and Masha raced out after him on to the stairs, where she tearfully told him all about her mother, her mother's lover, and the ruffians. The Muscovite took her back to his Party functionary's suite, and for five days they were inseparable. Masha followed him around everywhere. If he was giving a speech to miners, metalworkers or wounded solders, she sat in the hall with her happy eyes trained on him. Even if he was speaking to a small Party cell, she waited patiently in the lobby, paying no attention to the horrible overbearing secretaries.

It had once seemed to Masha that she was most important and that everything and everybody revolved around her. But now a man had turned up who was much more important. You couldn't even compare them! But this did not affect her pride. On the contrary – for the sake of this Muscovite she was willing to trample herself into the ground and become nothing, so long as he was with her. He was so enormous that he did not just shield Masha from misfortunes. He blocked out the whole world. Masha forgot all about Valyaba the Boxer, and her mother, and the partisan – that was how wonderful she felt. It was all so marvellous, so fine, that it was even frightening. Her head spun as though she was perched on the edge of an abyss . . . For between Masha and this man yawned a very real abyss. At night Masha clung to him and hugged him so that they almost merged together . . . And none the less there was an abyss between them . . .

Why? Because for her the Muscovite was everything – a dream, a hope, the future, the present, salvation, the very fulcrum of her life – whereas for him she was just a girl he bumped into. If it hadn't been Masha, another would have turned up – say, one of those painted bitches from the Party Committee.

At times Masha reminded herself of one of the little girls who presented Stalin with flowers on the reviewing stand at the May Day parades. They would choose a cute little Young Pioneer, photograph her for the newsreels and *Ogonyok* magazine, blind her with nationwide glory for a few days, then forget her for ever.

Well, Masha was prepared for anything. And it wasn't herself she was sorry for, but that forty-odd-year-old boy! Why did he drink so much? Was he really unaware of how wonderful he was? But he was killing himself with drink! Couldn't he stop? No one understood him – even his Moscow wife. He was probably very lonely with her, otherwise he would not drink so much and go with other women. Although it was they who flocked to him, really. He just had to glance at them and they were willing, and exploited the fact that he was tipsy. So how could she save him from drink? If only Masha could manage to do that; how grateful he would be, how he would love her for it. He would be happier with her than anyone had ever dreamt of being . . .

But then the Muscovite flew off in a military aircraft, and Masha humbly drifted home from the factory aerodrome. At home they ignored her. Her mother, swollen with tears and with a towel wound round her head, slouched about the flat like a tired witch. Her lover lay on the couch with a hot-water bottle, and resembled a football with a burst bladder. One did not even feel like kicking him.

Two days later they were both arrested.

Having escaped from his daughter, old Cholyshev stood irresolutely in the boulevard. He had no desire to go back to his wife. 'Soviet men,' he paraphrased Zhenya, 'don't like going to work in the mornings, or home at night.' And after all, visiting his deceased ex-wife had proved harder than the work he used to do, and at home he faced the prospect of Tokarev's memoirs being hammered out.

'As usual, there is no choice.' Cholyshev knitted his brow, and even the vibrant green Moscow boulevard seemed false, as though the tops of the trees were not wet with rain but had been specially sprinkled from a hose, like lettuce-leaves at the market.

'Should I go to the cinema? Or is the whole of our life not a cinema, where you just watch what is shown?!' The old man grinned lop-sidedly and trudged off in the direction of home, which was about fifteen kilometres away. There was no choice.

. . . There had never been a choice. Even on the eighth of May, when the soldiers bored rocket-holes in the Hungarian sky all night long. Cholyshev also saluted with his pistol and brushed tears of happiness from his eyes, and in the morning applied for demobilization. He had to hurry to Siberia and find out what had happened to Masha, who seemed to have vanished into thin air.

The application went off to be processed. But there were rumours that their unit was to be transferred to the Far East, and in the end the rumours overtook the application. The officers were moved out of private flats into barracks, and then they were all loaded into converted goods vans and dispatched across Europe to the back of beyond.

Just imagine you're Przhevalsky,* Cholyshev tried to cheer himself up. As a boy you didn't run off to America . . . so just lie back on your plank-bed, you're a government-sponsored traveller . . .

But when they had to make a break, beyond the Urals, to allow tanks and artillery to pass, Engineers' Captain Cholyshev went to the staff car, obtained five days' leave, and jumped on to a train carrying hooded ack-ack guns.

Bronka's town lay some five hundred kilometres south of the Trans-Siberian Railway. Alighting from a dirty local train, Cholyshev found himself on the metallurgical planet devised by Stalin at the end of the twenties.† The sun was setting behind gigantic foundries and blast-furnaces, making him feel like the last

---

*Nineteenth-century Russian traveller, explorer of Central Asia. [Tr.]
† The town is Stalinsk-Kuznetsk (now Novokuznetsk), rapidly developed in the First Five-Year Plan (1928–32) as a vast centre for the production of iron, steel and coal. [Tr.]

man on Earth in this civilian town. If Masha was in trouble, his soldier's credentials would cut no ice here.

They won't let me stay the night, anyway, thought Cholyshev as he sadly approached a grey seven-storey building, evidently built just before the war. Faced with granite at ground level, it stood out from the other buildings, which were three- and four-storey plastered or red-brick barracks, similar to those which Cholyshev had erected as a student. 'Council of People's Commissars,' he thought gloomily, not doubting that he would be asked to show a pass. But there was no doorman, nor any lift in the lift-shaft, and Pavel, taking courage, climbed the stairs to the fourth floor as though entering a fray.

The bell jangled sharply and impatiently, as if it had not been rung for a long time. She's in prison, thought Cholyshev, but then heard slow, heavy, disgruntled footsteps.

'Who's there?' asked a hoarse, indifferent voice behind the door, as though its owner no longer expected anything, good or bad, and was merely annoyed at having to tramp along the corridor and turn the lock.

'Open up. It's me.'

The captain's own voice sounded strange to him.

The tall, almost nine-feet-high door opened, and Bronka, with an enormous rounded belly, stood facing Cholyshev.

'Pashka! Where have you come from?'

Familyless, but in the family way . . . Cholyshev smiled sadly to himself, and asked: 'Where's Masha?'

'You're wasting your time. She's not here.'

'Where is the girl?'

'The whore, you mean . . .'

'I'll shoot you!' shouted Cholyshev. Bronka's face twisted with hatred.

'Don't bawl at me! My interrogator roared at me and I wasn't scared. Why should a pipsqueak like you scare me?'

Collecting himself, Cholyshev walked down the long corridor to the room and saw a large brown seal on the second door.

'Is that the partisan's?' he asked mockingly and at once turned red. 'Tell me what's happened to Masha? I can see you're in a mess, but spare a thought for me too. No letters for a year, then suddenly the girl wants to join me. So I send for her, and there's silence . . . I hear she was plagued to death by your Lazo,* may he burn in a furnace!'

'He was killed in the cells . . . And your daughter buggered off to Moscow. I send her your money, though she doesn't give a curse for it. Do you know who she's with?'

'Tell me . . .'

'Her first "cavalier" – handsome, at that, though he's a Muscovite bastard. It was because of him that we suffered.'

'But . . . but the girl's only sixteen!'

'Was I any older, do you remember?'

'Is she pregnant?'

'Good God, no. He's got sense, not like you.'

'Tell me about Masha.'

'Hold on. Someone's knocking. Must be a friend . . .'

Bronka shuffled out into the hall. She was wearing slippers on her bare feet.

'What's brought you here? Come in. You're just in time to stop me being killed.'

'You're joking, Varvara Alekseyevna. How are you, better?' asked a low female voice.

'I shan't get any better now, Nadka. If the comrade captain doesn't shoot me I'll die in childbirth.'

Bronka ushered a tall, dark-haired woman into the room.

'Shall I introduce you, or do you remember him?'

'I remember,' said the woman in an embarrassed voice. 'Varvara Alekseyevna, Grisha leaves in the morning. You promised some salami . . .' she said shyly.

'Yes, I've got some. I was saving it to hand in to Mikhail Stepanich, but there's no need now . . . You'll find it in the kitchen. Do you know what, Pashka – her brother fell madly in love with

* Soviet partisan burned by the Japanese in a steam-engine. [Tr.]

our Masha, but she didn't give a shit about him. So he found himself someone else – an exiled convict.'*

'Why do you speak like that, Varvara Alekseyevna? You know there's nothing between them. Grisha's just a boy, and Zheka's seen enough to make her sick of men.'

'Well, I don't suppose they're exactly throwing themselves at her, either,' Bronka smiled wryly. 'Did you take the sausage? If you're going now, take this officer with you. You can tell him how Masha is set up in Moscow. I'm going to lie down; I'm exhausted. Let him carry the salami. Or do you have a bag? Of course you do – the only place a woman goes without a bag these days is to the bath or to bed . . .'

The windows and street-lights of the garden-city glorified *in absentia* by Mayakovsky† were shining peacefully, and even the dusty foliage gave off a dull gleam, but it all still irritated Cholyshev. Nadya Tokar walked beside him in silence.

She probably thinks Bronka has palmed me off on her for the night, thought Cholyshev angrily. You're wrong, my dear. Just tell me quickly what Masha's doing, and I'll get back to the station. I don't have time to hang about . . .

Realizing, however, that he wasn't going to hear anything very comforting, he did not hurry her, and she showed no desire to delve into someone else's life.

'What a situation . . .' Cholyshev sighed. 'You can't get by without bimber . . .'

'What's bimber?' she asked.

'Polish moonshine.'

'We don't have any. Only vodka,' said Nadya. 'But whenever Zheka and I get any, on the ration cards, we

* It was and still is Soviet penal practice for a term in a labour-camp to be followed by exile to a remote region of the Soviet Union. [Tr.]

† Inspired by a conversation with a worker from Kuznetsk, Vladimir Mayakovsky wrote a poem celebrating the development of the city as a great feat of engineering and human endeavour. The poem includes the words: 'Here, within four years, will be a garden city.' [Tr.]

exchange it for something else.'

'Who's Zheka? The convict?' asked Cholyshev, without any real interest.

'Yes. She was let out under the amnesty. No, she's not a criminal . . . It's just that her sentence was only five years. She was in because of her parents . . . So you've been liberating Poland? No? Pity. I'm interested in what it's like there. A Polish friend of mine wants me to go there with him. No, he wasn't at the front: he hurt himself against a chest when he was small and his leg didn't grow properly. He's got golden hands, though: made a new bobbin for me. And his head, as my aunt used to say, is nothing short of Jewish. He's very clever, but he doesn't want to stay here. He thinks the USSR's no place for a hard-working person. We haven't learned how to work, he says. I argue with him – I mean, look at the patriotism there was! In the factories they were putting in twelve hours a day or more for the war effort. He just laughs: he says that was a disgrace, not work. And you can't change his mind. I was taught differently, but Alf – he's called Alfred – Alf says: if they won't let you work for yourself here, then there's no point in living here either. And he also believes they'll straighten out his leg properly abroad. Medicine's quite different over there.'

'I see you think of the West as some kind of paradise,' said Cholyshev.

'Not at all! More as some kind of hospital! So you also think it's not right to leave your motherland? I've thought a lot about what that means to me. "Motherland", "fatherland" – for most people it's where their family is, but all I've got left is one brother, Grisha. And he's struck out on his own. He even changed the name in his passport from Tokar to Tokarev, so that it sounds Russian. He wants to become a writer, and a writer can't live abroad, where the language is different. But it doesn't matter to me what language they speak. I'd like to have a baby . . .'

Cholyshev was surprised at how open-hearted she was being. The woman was beginning to amuse him.

'The doctors here don't know much . . .' she sighed, and then hurriedly added: 'Oh, I'm sorry. I keep talking about myself, and you're interested in Masha. Don't you worry about her. Everything's going very well for her. Of course, she's still young, but to look at her – you wouldn't believe it – she's perfectly grown-up. She was always like a princess at the dances. It was awful, there used to be riots over her.'

'Tough guys?'

'You get all sorts at the dances ... Varvara Alekseyevna pobably exaggerated things in her annoyance. It's just nerves. Mikhail Stepanich was a big shot – he had two secretaries in front of his office. And suddenly – he ends up in prison ...' The woman gave a sigh.

She's remembered her father, Cholyshev decided ... Although they'd scarcely have held him along with ordinary criminals: they'd have shot him straight after the interrogation.

'Maybe Mikhail Stepanich raised his voice to them, and gangsters don't like that,' said Nadya.

'And what did they arrest him for?'

'There are different stories. He and Varvara Alekseyevna fed the whole town, and no one starved. Of course, they looked after themselves too. What do you expect? It's just people like my mother who could care for others without asking anything for herself. And she didn't live long. My friend Zheka is like that too ... But everyone thinks about themselves. Probably there were people who were envious of Mikhail Stepanich. Varvara Alekseyevna thinks he was arrested to give evidence against his old friend, a big Moscow leader.'

'The one who's now with my daughter?'

'Yes ... But that's not so bad, Comrade Captain. It's good, in fact ... I knew him once – he's a very warm and cheerful person, although his work is difficult and he has scores of enviers. But he will help your Masha a lot. He may not be young himself, but he understands young people.'

'Especially girls?'

'That's life, Comrade Captain ... Would it have been better if she had taken up with thugs? She used to go around with them, you know. As it is she'll go to university, she'll be surrounded by cultured people. If you knew how my Zheka misses them! In Moscow she had lots of like-minded friends, but here there's only Grisha for her to talk literature with.'

After wandering though unlit alleys between shanties, mud huts and sheds, Nadya and the captain stopped before a magnificent pool, straight from the Ukrainian countryside, behind which stood a lonely, crooked little house. This was evidently where the town ended. Only the black outlines of waste heaps loomed in the distance.

'Careful,' warned the woman. 'You have to walk on the planks.'

'I thought your Pole was good with his hands. Can't he drain off this puddle?'

'Oh, there's a pipe here that bursts three times a day. Alf wants me to move in with him. He's got a better room. When his brother moves out I'll go there. But I must see Zheka married first.'

'Your friend comes first?' said Cholyshev with a smile. He had taken a liking to the young woman. She was responsive and natural, the kind of person you could spend an age with even without love. It was a shame that in her foolish youth she had injured herself messing about in Bronka's hotel.

'It's true, she comes first,' she said sadly. 'We've been together a year and a half – who knows if I'd last that long with a husband! But Zheka – she really needs to get married. She's got nobody else. If I go it will be the end of her. She ought to leave first. Anything could happen to her . . . She wouldn't survive a second term. As it is she's in a state. Rushes about like a bird in a cage. Now she wants to enter medical college, because doctors have an easier time in the camps. Oh, my tongue is wagging so much – we've arrived . . .'

Nadya Tokar led Cholyshev into a dark little corridor, pushed one of three doors, and turned on the light. Cholyshev looked round the room. It was partitioned in the middle by a tall stove. Next to the stove hung a flowery sheet, not reaching the ground, under which the legs of a wooden bedstead protruded. Two more bedsteads were lined up on this side of the curtain; on one of them lay an old suitcase, and between them, in pride of place, was a sewing machine on a home-made stand.

The Pole must have knocked it together for her, thought Cholyshev, suddenly envying the cosiness of the room, which, though it seemed intolerably poor, at least bore a resemblance to a human dwelling. All the captain had was a plank-bunk in a freight-car, and that freight-car was now either crawling on past Novosibirsk or was still waiting in a siding to let those who mattered more pass.

'You're probably hungry?' said the woman. 'We'll have some supper.'

'Certainly,' Cholyshev nodded, and started emptying the contents of his kitbag on to the table: a loaf of bread, cans of food, bars of millet concentrate, and finally a small canister. Nadya stared in shock at the solider, imagining him gorging himself with food and drink, and then – who knows?! – shooting himself . . .

Something similar must have flashed through Cholyshev's mind, for, after emptying his kitbag, he stood up with a wry smile, took his hostess's arm, and cried: 'So where is my son-in-law that never was? Wouldn't he care to take a drink with his fool of a father-in-law?'

Here we go . . . thought Nadya with horror, already regretting having brought home the father of such a destructive influence as Masha. They all ran after Masha, even the grey-haired Muscovite. Whereas he did not even recognize Nadya at first when she went up to him after his talk in the city theatre. He did, it is true, at least blush with embarrassment (only he could blush in such a boyish way, all over his thin, ever-young face) and started apologizing: 'Well, of course, how should I recognize you when you – despite, as it were, the hardships of wartime – are so beautiful?! You were pretty as a girl too, but not compared with how you are now. You're really not married? Ah, of course, the war . . . But you do have a boyfriend! Some lads on the home front have all the luck. And where's your little brother? Do you remember how the little devil looked into the lumber-room? In the top form at school? Writing articles? Quite right: his poetry was no use at all. Tell him to pop in and see me at the Party Committee. I'd invite you too, of course, but I wouldn't like to make your home-front comrade jealous . . .'

The Muscovite praised Grisha's article about wartime prose, and also approved his decision to amend his name.

'All the Soviet people are Russians now. Only Russians could win such a terrible war,' he said, and wrote – on Central Committee notepaper – a letter of recommendation to the Literary Institute of Soviet Writers.

. . . And just when everything has turned out right I have to bring this nutcase here, thought Nadya Tokar now.

Suddenly the curtain jerked and revealed a young woman in a grey skirt and a blue man's shirt which was not buttoned up to the top. Her cropped auburn hair and small wire-framed spectacles gave her an immature, almost schoolgirlish appearance. Cholyshev felt a shiver of pity, and at once gave a smile so that his pity would not show on his face.

'Excuse me, please,' he said in embarrassment, and launched into a stream of tactless nonsense: 'What a stroke of bad luck. I once saw an optician's shop in Austria. The owner had fled and there were glasses there with frames of every description imaginable, like in some communist paradise. If I'd known I'd have brought some . . .'

'Hmm,' Nadya sighed, thinking the captain was mocking her friend.

'So I'm out of luck?' said the young woman with a nod of her head. 'What's that you've got?' she asked, looking at the dark-red canister. 'Is it explosive?'

'Plum brandy. Never mind, I'll know next time. Give me the lens numbers and I'll send send you them from Japan.'

'Zheka, this is Masha's father,' said Nadya.

'I'd guessed.'

'Am I like her?' asked Cholyshev.

'Fortunately not very,' said Zheka with an ironic smile, and Cholyshev took offence.

The door squeaked and a thin youth with black hair in the Mayakovsky style came in. He gave the captain a unfriendly nod.

What a fool I am, thought Cholyshev, and he glanced at Zheka. Behind the little lenses, her eyes seemed to be looking right through him. Not that there was anything very mysterious about him . . . A victor had come rushing to save his daughter, but she had skipped off to Moscow to become the concubine of a high Party apparatchik. So the victor gate-crashed on somebody else's hovel, on somebody else's life, somebody else's farewell party.

Did I have a choice, then, or is there never any choice? wondered the old man many long years later. If I had not met Zhenya in that shanty, it is hardly likely that I would have tried to catch up with my unit. The Japanese campaign did not interest me. In that July after the victory I imagined I was quite unfit for anything any more. The Lord must have sent me Zhenya that night so that I would not empty a pistol into my head . . .

But meanwhile Zhenya sat quietly at the table opposite the captain, and her eyes watched him through her schoolgirl's glasses, bewildered and perturbed. Nadya realized that *something* was happening between her friend and Masha's father, and involuntarily felt sad. She even conversed listlessly: 'It's probably not really that much fun in Poland. The towns have been destroyed. In Warsaw not a single house was left untouched.'

'Oh, forget Warsaw for once, Nadka! We're saying goodbye. For ever and ever!' The youth suddenly hugged his sister and started crying.

'He oughtn't to drink,' Cholyshev whispered to Zheka.

'Who's he to give orders! Zheka, tell him to stop bossing people about!' said the youth angrily.

'Calm down, Grishka, the captain was only joking. Weren't you, Pavel Rodionovich? Our Grishka is grown-up and independent. He can drink a lot. He's just not in the mood at the moment,' said Nadka, trying to console her brother.

Zheka remained silent, as before, as though everything in the world – the camp, exile, the boy's crying – meant no more to her than the empty walls and the bare stove, or the carelessly laid planks over the pool. As though behind all this flowed Zheka's invisible, closed life, which Pavel Cholyshev could not understand or penetrate. Zheka herself, on the other hand, not only penetrated Cholyshev and divined his past, but even grasped the present shaky hopes which had suddenly surfaced in him. And Zheka's eyes seemed to admonish the captain: 'I understand, it's hard for you. You were used to caring for someone, and now there is nobody. That's why you started blabbing about the glasses, before you'd even said hello . . . No, I'm not offended. It's pleasant. Nobody has taken care of me for a long time. But for Heaven's sake, don't look on me as your destiny. I don't even know what to do with my own destiny. Yet you stare at me as if I were your salvation . . .'

'Don't get upset, Grishka,' Nadya repeated. 'Pavel Rodionovich won't boss Zheka round. Zheka will come away with us.'

'There's a second Pole who's got his eye on her,' the youth smiled through his tears.

'There's no need to tell me that. I'm an outsider.' Cholyshev's face darkened. He saw that it was time for his hostess to get her brother ready for the road, but still he did not get up, and sat drinking plum brandy, unable to take his eyes off Zheka. Time was so compressed that it seemed it could explode at any moment. At harvest-time, a few days feed a year, and here a second could overturn Cholyshev's fate. More and more blatantly he drank in Zheka's face, her neck, barely covered in blue fustian, and her arms, bared to the elbows, and overflowed with pity for this little girl. The air around her breathed, and the space between them was tense with thunderstorm discharges.

The door squeaked again and a lean man came in. Looks foreign, thought Cholyshev: there's nothing Jewish in his face.

'Come in, please!' he said, jumping to his feet and offering food and drink. The man, who had come in with a sad smile, looked at the tipsy soldier, and Cholyshev suddenly felt ill at ease. During the last two years of the offensive he had grown accustomed to hospitality being offered not by the owners of a house or hut but by those who brought the food.

'Why does he keep giving orders?' sobbed the youth again.

'Sit down, Alf.' Nadya pushed a stool out from under the table.

'I'm not suited for peacetime,' Cholyshev whispered to Zheka.

'Yes you are . . .' she replied, even more quietly.

'Have a drink, Alf. It's plum brandy,' said Nadya. 'The comrade captain is just passing through . . . Oh, this strong stuff makes me feel like singing!'

Suddenly a guitar, not unlike Nadya Tokar herself, appeared on her knees, and she began singing in a low voice 'My Campfire Shines in the Mist', but not in the romance style – like Tchaikovsky's version – nor in the gypsy style, but in a much more rollicking, open style.

She must have learned to sing like that at Bronka's hotel, thought Cholyshev, but then the song took hold of him as though he and Zheka were the wandering gypsies being sung about. But the gypsies in the song 'came together like the knotted points of your shawl', whereas Zheka and he had merely been looking at each other across a table for a couple of hours.

> . . . Who tomorrow, my falcon,
> Will undo the knot
> That you tied on my breast?

Perhaps Nadya's song was a hint that it was time for Cholyshev to be moving on? But what knot was there to speak of? It wasn't he who had tied the knot, and it was some other Pole who was undoing it. He would shove Zheka into a passenger train and take her not to China, but to Poland or even further . . . While Pavel would beat his fist against his plank-bed and mumble 'On the Hills of Manchuria'. How he wanted to stay! He was not a gypsy, after all! Let Alf take Nadya away, and this cry-baby go to Moscow, and let Zheka wait for him here! Only . . . would he return? What luck, eh? – Having got through a war like that, to drag yourself off to the next, pointless one!

Remember me when someone else . . .

No, I've decided, there won't be anyone else. Either Zheka or nobody . . .

After 'My Campfire', Nadya struck up another song, 'Shine, Shine, My Star', but at the most pathetic moment she let the guitar fall from her knees and it struck the floor with a plaintive twang.

'Oi, Pavel Rodionovich has fallen in love,' she laughed. 'Love at first sight! I haven't met a man like that for ages!'

At this something snapped inside Cholyshev. Suffusing with blood, he cut his hostess with a hostile look and got up.

'It's time for me to go. Thanks for the shelter!' He wanted to sound severe, but it came out shrill, like a cock crowing, and the captain picked up his now thin kitbag and hurried out of the room. He felt injured and depressed. Why does everything in life end in odious failure? Nadka Tokar – either from imprudence or from malice – had slashed those invisible threads that were already stretching between Zheka and Cholyshev. 'It's as if she had exposed an undeveloped film,' he thought absent-mindedly, and pushed the sloping door.

'Captain, wait. I'll accompany you . . .' said Zheka's soft voice behind him, and the room became as quiet as if everything had flown out of it through the stove-pipe.

(She chose, not me, Cholyshev sometimes reflected, and now, in the Moscow boulevard, he thought of it again. She was promised the West, but she stayed behind to wait for me, even though she could not know that the Manchurian campaign would turn out to be a short one, that the Americans would drop a bomb on

Hiroshima and it would end up more like an excursion than a war. But I did bring her back a whole suitcase full of spectacles! I didn't have time to ask at the station what kind she needed. A freight train was passing and I jumped into the brake-van, though I desperately wanted to stay. Zheka had a look on her face as though we had just been intimate. Shy, cultured, delicately organized women always have rather embarrassed faces early in the morning – as though they had slept through their stop in the night and were travelling without a ticket.)

The old man was deeply moved by this flood of memories, and now the boulevard looked perfectly normal to him again: an ordinary late-afternoon boulevard. There was a June freshness in the trees and Cholyshev, throwing off the years, suddenly missed his wife. He ran across the road, waved down a passing car, and was soon opening his own front door.

Zhenya was sitting in the kitchen reading a letter.

'They've taken Varvara Alekseyevna away. Tokarev's just phoned.' Her voice seemed to contain a reprimand: why did you not wait for the undertakers?

'Oh he did, did he? They'll soon take me away too . . .' growled the old man.

'Pashet, stop it.'

'Either you're typing him, or he's phoning . . . Tokarev, Tokarev, it never stops. There's no peace.'

'Pashet, your wife has died, and that's all you can talk about.'

'She died too late . . . I should have shot her back in Siberia.'

'That's stupid. What would I have done if you'd been sent to the camps?'

'Gone to America.'

'You should be ashamed of yourself. Read this, by the way. Nadya is asking us again to visit her. It's becoming almost awkward to keep turning her down. Shall we go?'

'You go on your own.'

'I'd like to see me try!'

He took the letter and, holding it some distance from his eyes, read: ' "Dear Zheka and Pavel Rodionovich! I miss you terribly..." What rubbish! It's sheer affectation.'

'Pashet, she hasn't anybody to speak Russian with there.'

'Neither have I ... Neither Russian nor anything else!' shouted the old man and stormed out of the room. Nadya's letters always unsettled him, but just now he was thinking that there was no need for his wife to go and visit her old friend. She could easily defect to the United States.

The bureau was closed. There were no traces of Tokarev.

'... You should have married a real woman, Pashet. You would have blocked out the whole world for her.' The old man remembered Zhenya's comment that morning. Yes – he said to himself – I didn't carry her away. I wonder what share of her heart I can lay claim to?

'Pashet, it's just amazing,' Zhenya laughed in the kitchen. 'You are over seventy, but you rage like a little boy. How many pent-up emotions there are in you!'

She went into the living-room, embraced her husband, and he yielded again, overwhelmed more by the warmth of her hands than by her words.

'All the same, I think I shall go to America. It seems to be a realistic proposition at the moment. For some reason I'd love to see Nadya again. You'll cope without me. Now ...' She faltered, referring to Varvara Alekseyevna's death. 'Now you have less to worry about ... I'm sorry to bring this up now, but I'm afraid that if I wait it might be too late.'

'You're still young,' whispered the old man and buried his face in her shoulder.

'No one knows when they will die,' sighed Zhenya, and Cholyshev remembered that Masha's long-haired friend had said the same thing in the afternoon.

Nobody knows the hour of their death, thought Zhenya. But sometimes one senses the approach of disaster almost physically.

Why should I fly to America? To show Pashet what a free woman I am? Why not come clean, that I want to live for a few months without seeing that sullen physiognomy and that cantankerous character?

She glanced gingerly at her husband. He was lying on the day-bed with his back turned, and Zhenya could not tell whether he was angry or dozing. He's old, she thought, and soon he'll be senile. Our life is over, and there will be no next one. Am I old? No. (She shook her head and, as always, a wiry lock of hair fell girlishly on to her cheek.) No . . . I am hoping for something. Old age is a surrender to the past, and I am still waiting for something – or rather, I am running from myself, and there is no peace for me anywhere . . . It's because I am trying to race against my age. But you'll never fool anyone that way. It would be far more honest to leave Pashet instead of returning to him every time as though nothing had happened . . . No – she interrupted herself – I did not go away for long, only for a few hours at a time. It wasn't serious, just a breath of fresh air. Otherwise I could not have held out . . . Nothing is ever right for Pashet. And he's as suspicious as a camp security guard. No, he is just old. I left him *for a short time*. But I never intended to desert him . . . What if I am just a coward? A coward and a deceiver? After all, I decided to escape to America . . . not escape, but go there for two months. When Nadya sends an official invitation I'll go. It's possible these days. Although they may not let out former jail-birds. But I'll manage somehow! (Zhenya felt angry.) Enough of this vacillation! I will get a visa and go there, before it's too late. Sciatica, angina, cardiac insufficiency, nervous exhaustion . . . Look at everything that's wrong with me! Why do I need Nadya? It's almost thirty years since we last saw each other, so there must be some good reason. Perhaps I haven't long left and I went to refresh my memories. And Nadya is one of my dearest memories . . .

First-year languages student Zhenya Knysh was arrested with her parents. A quiet Moscow girl, she had no skills before camp and learnt none in camp. For about half a year she shoved trolleys at a brick-works. And then disaster struck. She got pregnant by a young doctor's assistant, a former medical student.

'I'll talk to the doctors about it. They may agree,' he tried to reassure Zhenya, and also himself.

'Don't talk nonsense. Abortions are prohibited even outside the zone. You'll do it yourself.'

'But I've only ever dissected corpses,' exclaimed the frightened student.

'Well, I'm certainly not going to have a kid in camp. I'd rather hang myself,' said Zhenya, realizing that she only had herself to count on.

She started lifting heavier loads of bricks than the most frenzied Stakhanovite. She had to hurry, for she was afraid of growing to love the child within her, which would in any case be taken away from her. But her young body disdained hunger, lack of sleep, and sickness, and her stomach grew rounder and rounder . . .

She had already lost hope when the bleeding began. There was, of course, no transport in the zone, and Zhenya had to be carried to the medical hut. When she was laid out on the table, even the elderly woman doctor, who was used to the fantastic way in which women cling to life, was astounded that Zhenya had not died.

She was officially invalided, and allowed to work as a nurse in the medical unit, and no sooner was her five-year term up than she as turfed out. With the war on, hardly anybody was being set free. But Zhenya bore scant resemblance to a living woman. It is unlikely that she would have lasted long had she not chanced to meet Nadya Tokar. Nadya nursed her back to health and almost got her to emigrate with her. Alf's friend, also a Polish Jew, was considering whether to marry Zheka, but Zheka gave him no encouragement whatsoever.

'What's the point of humming and hawing?' Nadya scolded her friend. 'Without us you're done for, and no captain's going to help you. He doesn't even write to you. Either he's been killed or he's changed his mind. And anyway, there was never anything between you for him to start writing letters. But you just need to give *him* a wink (she meant the Polish Jew) and he's ready . . .'

'I'm not going to do the dirty on a decent bloke like him,' Zhenya replied. 'What if they don't let me out? What then?'

'Pah, the bullet fears the brave, they say . . .' said Nadya dismissively.

'But I don't want to spoil things for you anyway,' Zheka replied. 'No, you go alone.'

And they did go.

It was a cold and hungry autumn that soon set in, because the Tokars, in anticipation of their departure, had laid in neither potatoes nor fuel. The shanty was as draughty as a labour-camp barrack, and time dragged by even more sadly than in the zone. But in November, on one typical evening without hope, came a delicate knock at the door, and there on the step stood Cholyshev, ear-flaps down, his kitbag on his back, and in each hand a suitcase . . . Zhenya hugged him, whirled round, and for the first time rejoiced that she had not married the Pole. Out there in Europe such miracles were impossible . . .

Now her life really did take a miraculous turn. She grew better-looking by the day. Everyone noticed it – neighbours, fellow students, even nodding acquaintances. It was as if the air of freedom, unmuzzled, had broken down a cell-door and invaded Zhenya Knysh's destiny. The shanty was surrounded, as ever, by the plains of Siberia, but even Siberia seemed somehow warmer. As a matter of fact, the thought of moving away from Siberia was frightening. Only a common criminal like Varvara Alekseyevna could allow herself that. After having given birth to her child, she scurried back to her home town, resumed her Party activities, and soon moved to Moscow.

Sometimes Pashet's work took him to Moscow, but he always returned angry and depressed, as though everything connected with the capital drove him out of his wits. Zhenya guessed that he was dissatisfied with his daughter.

It was true that Masha's life did not please Cholyshev. There was no high Party functionary anywhere near her. She was always either getting divorced or getting married, and her room, which was constantly full of noisy, drunk and dissolute men, looked like a railway station or a hotel. Cutting short his trips, Pashet would escape from this horror to Siberia, to his dear, quiet, affectionate Zhenya, and there was no cosier corner on Earth for him than that hovel on the outskirts of town – and later their two-roomed flat in the centre.

But then the Generalissimus died, and Zhenya Knysh, as though awakening from a long Siberian hibernation, became thinner-faced, younger, and rebellious.

'Moscow! We must go to Moscow!' she repeated day in day out. 'If we don't go now, we'll never go . . .'

She began writing to awe-inspiring Moscow departments and searching for friends of her father and her own former friends, and Cholyshev observed apprehensively how Zhenya was transforming herself from a cowed and submissive deportee into a determined, courageous and, most important of all, self-sufficient woman. Would she not remain so in Moscow? For in Moscow Pavel would not be able to help her in any way. Would she not end up alone, exposed and without support? Would she not turn into one of those capital-city martyrs, worn out by the Moscow crowds and distances, constantly tearing herself apart between work, queues and home? And if in Moscow he and Zhenya became embittered with one another and family life became a bitter wrangle . . .?

Cholyshev tried to persuade his wife of the fragility of the new policy of rehabilitation. The policy had not been publicly announced, after all. More than that: *Pravda* had recently called Khrushchev's secret speech* an invention of Western propaganda, although it had been read to non-Party people. Not that there was anything surprising about that. The Party could not be expected to repent, and its dignitaries, exposed as criminals, would not trudge through the streets of Moscow like German prisoners of war, to

* His famous anti-Stalinist speech to the Party Congress in 1956, never published in the USSR. [Tr.]

the glory of justice and for the edification of posterity. No power would allow itself any such luxury.

But Zhenya was immovable, and Cholyshev found himself climbing to the top bunk of a railway compartment. The journey promised to be a pleasant one. They were travelling light, like newly-weds. Zhenya was as delighted as a schoolgirl breaking out of some provincial backwater for the first time, and the only thing that distressed her was the prospect of being met at Moscow's Kazan Station by her step-daughter.

But all of a sudden a fat bustling woman barged into the compartment and roared in a policeman's voice: 'Chelyshev! Where is he? Come here, Chelyshev!'

Pavel, somewhat startled, unfolded a telegram: VERY SORRY CANNOT MEET YOU STOP RING ME IN EVENING LOVE MASHA.

No fear; let her look for us, thought Zhenya, though she felt sorry for her husband. Even before, he had sat staring out of the window with knitted brows, as though he were being transported away in the opposite direction, and under escort at that. And now, after the telegram, he looked like a condemned man.

I tempted Pashet to Moscow by saying he would be able to see his daughter more often, thought Zhenya. But it turns out she doesn't need her father at all.

Only in the evening, when the radio announced the suicide of Masha's former lover, did Pashet come to life a little. Zhenya, on the other hand, became uneasy; something unforeseen had clearly happened in the capital. Could her wise husband have been right? There it was: the first death. But those people rarely committed suicide. Why did he do it? Out of fear? No, that would not be like him . . .

She remembered how long ago Nadya and Grisha had taken her to the town theatre to hear a talk by the eminent Moscow propagandist. Although many of the audience were wearing padded jackets, Zhenya felt even more uncomfortable in the theatre than the day before in the miners' club. It seemed to her that everyone knew who she was, and that she would shortly be removed from the hall. It would be something, indeed, if that was the worst that came of it. She would never have gone there – nor to the dance the previous evening – had it not been for Grisha Tokarev. How could she deny it: she would have followed Tokarev anywhere at all . . . However, she ought not to be thinking about Tokarev just now, but about the Moscow apparatchik. Why did he shoot himself?

That day at the theatre Zhenya actually found him appealing, although his voice was rather high for a man's. On the other hand he did not give himself airs, and was not even remotely like either the prison bosses or the town's bigwigs. He did not speak from notes, and spoke of Stalin, Roosevelt, Churchill and the Soviet marshals in a down-to-earth way, as one would of friends or neighbours. His only fault was a too frequent use of the expression 'so to say'. Zhenya wondered how this grey-haired man would have conducted himself if he had been appointed head of a camp or a district soviet.

Better than most, she decided now in the train. He did have some kind of decency in him. He was certainly being watched. To intimidate him they arrested his partisan friend, Varvara Alekseyevna's lover, but he got cold feet. He even helped Tokarev, though he knew Tokarev's father had been shot. Why should a person like that take his own life? Was he afraid of a Soviet Nuremberg Trial? But it's obvious that there is not the faintest likelihood of any such thing – I agree absolutely with Pashet on that. However, suicide is a bold step, there's no getting away from it. Perhaps it was a kind of catharsis – a cleansing of someone who did not believe in God and immortality. However it was, it is all very sad. He was not the worst in their gang, and I shall certainly feel no joy if they start taking poison or shooting themselves like Goerings. Pangs of conscience are all very well, but I would rather that man had gone on living, and Masha, instead of attending his funeral, would be waiting for us at Kazan Station, and we would kiss each other like two subdued viragos . . .

After lugging their suitcases to a taxi-rank and waiting their turn in a long queue, Zhenya and Pavel finally found temporary accommodation. They were exhausted by the early heat, but had scarcely had time to recover their breath before Masha and Tokarev rolled into the room – young, happy, and tipsy, as though just back from the wedding office, not the cemetery.

Zhenya was disheartened. Why hadn't Tokarev written that he was meeting Pashet's daughter? In all his letters he complained untiringly that could not find work, that he was not being published, and was generally in a sorry plight. But it turned out he was perfectly happy.

After kissing her father Masha generously reached out to embrace her step-mother, but Zhenya merely shook her head.

. . . But Masha deserved pity. That day had not been easy for her. She could not have avoided going to the funeral.

Eleven years earlier, when her mother and her mother's lover were arrested, Masha had telephoned Moscow, sure that her handsome grey-haired friend would hang up on her. But he had sombrely told her she could go to Moscow, and sent her – *poste restante* – a pass for entry to the capital.

Masha hurriedly completed the documents, fearing that she would be summoned as a witness and required to give a written undertaking not to leave the town. Boxer lay in wait for her at every corner, hung around the entrance of her house, and in the end broke into the flat.

'Right! This time you won't turn away. You'll be mine . . .' He was breathing repulsively as he pressed Masha into the kitchen. The other rooms were sealed.

'Has that grey creep been screwing you?'

'Hold on, you silly,' Masha whispered, as though they were being overheard. She had to cool him off. Choking with tears, she swore that she was pure and that the grey-haired man had never done anything like that to her. It was her mother's lover who had kept thrusting himself on her, and the Muscovite, on the contrary, had hidden her at his place because her mother's lover was round the twist. And when the Muscovite went away, her mother's lover had raped her.

'I can't even fend you off, and look at what a great huge bull he is!' sobbed Masha, almost believing her own story.

Valyaba Boxer wept like a child. At one moment he was brutally beating Masha, at the next he was kissing her and swearing that the head of the Workers' Supplies Board would not escape him. He had mates in the jug . . . Masha could not wait to edge him out on to the landing.

That very evening, without saying goodbye to anyone, Masha squeezed into a packed train, and a week later she was met at the Kazan Station by the Muscovite's friend, Susanna Fyodorovna. Susanna sent her to classes, asked no questions, and merely made sure that Masha ate, washed and laundered her clothes regularly.

After two months the elderly woman suddenly announced: 'You can write to your mother now. She's been let out, but Mikhail Stepanich was killed by his cell-mates.'

That night Masha tried in vain to cry, and in the morning she sent her mother a short letter asking her to send her father's money to her care of the main post ofice and not to tell anyone where she, Masha, was. She was fed up with her Siberian acquaintances. In August Masha passed the final school examinations, and a month later the university entrance examinations. She moved into a student hostel on Stromynka Street and lost touch with Susanna Fyodorovna.

No, Masha could not have avoided going to the funeral . . .

The coffin was displayed in the main hall, and the line of those who craved to stand for a moment by the body stretched into the next one. There proved to be no fewer of them than there were ordinary mortals who came in off the street. On the dais, the widow was bending over the dead man, adjusting something, and smoothing his thin, white, combed-back hair and yellow cheeks.

She's working for her audience, thought Masha.

The last month and a half had seen a revival of Masha's affair with her benefactor, or rather, a debauched spree. Masha had just been left by her fourth husband, and her benefactor – moved from a position of power to one of honour – had ample leisure. Even under Stalin, by the way, he had managed to indulge in fortnight-long binges, unloading his most unpleasant engagements on to his meek comrades.

Today they were in charge of the funeral arrangements. Since Masha could not stand next to the widow or sit with the relatives in front of the coffin, she was allowed to jump to the head of the moving queue several times.

Suddenly a boy appeared on the dais beside the widow. Clinging to his mother, he looked in fear at the dead man, as though expecting a telling-off from him. The boy unsettled Masha, and she decided not to go up to the coffin again.

The line of mourners in the neigbouring hall, which looped and twisted several times, had turned into a regular scrum. Well, of course! How can you sit at home when a man has carried out his own execution?!

He was over-hasty, thought Masha. In his drunkenness he thought he was in hot water. He was a clever man, but behaved like a little boy. He left me alone . . . Masha burst into tears.

Masha's circumstances were certainly a cause for anxiety. It was now pointless trying to defend the dissertation which she had been writing for three years, since in its two hundred pages she had quoted Stalin forty-four times.

As if I could have got away with less! No, I'll have to wave goodbye to the dissertation. Even if *he* was alive (that is, her benefactor) I couldn't have defended it. Anyway, what weight did he pull recently? If he had done, he wouldn't have killed himself . . . What on earth am I thinking of?! I am alive. I shall write a new dissertation . . . Masha heaved a sigh, pulled off her arm-band, and went through to the third hall, which was less crowded.

Here, to the muted weeping of a distant wind orchestra, intellectuals and Party high priests sat around or scurried gloomily from corner to corner, separate from the other mourners. One or two of them nodded nonchalantly to Masha. But most of them turned away, and Masha again felt belittled and left out, as she had done in her childhood near the Party Secretary's house. She wanted to get away from all these important men and arrogant women, from the red- and green-curtained mirrors, and from the slow, brassy sobbing that reverberated inside her. But she had to stand and keep her chin up, although her shoes, bought the previous day, pinched her feet, and her heart ached like a sore tooth. How much better to be at Kazan Station in battered sandals, waiting patiently for an interminably delayed passenger train. Masha imagined her father and step-mother rushing up and down the platform looking for porters, and the thought discomforted her.

Zhenya is probably still annoyed with me because of the dance, she thought. But my father, bless him, deserved to be met by me. Trust their arrival to coincide with the funeral! What I need is a good weep on his shoulder. He loves me. He doesn't see me in the same light as these people do . . .

Masha looked round the hall again, and imagined she saw nothing but personal enemies. They were probably whispering about her: 'She's pretty, but depraved – you can see it in her eyes. She's insatiable . . . terrible . . .' But her father pitied her: he knew she was just a luckless fool, she thought, feeling sorry for herself. Suddenly she spotted Susanna Fyodorovna and Grishka in a far corner. Susanna had grown quite decrepit, but Grishka's appearance was remarkably unchanged since his Siberian days, or even since before the war, although he was now approaching thirty.

Why didn't I remember about him? thought Masha with surprise, and immediately, as though her shoes were not pinching and she were not at a funeral, as though they had only parted the day before, she smartly and provocatively, as if wishing to annoy all those pompous men and envious women, crossed the watchful hall, nodded carelessly to the old woman, and loudly addressed an embarrassed Grisha as though they were alone: 'Thank goodness I found you. They're arriving today. I don't know who will meet them.'

'Never mind. They'll find their own way,' mumbled Tokarev.

'And then how will I find them? They're staying with some friend of . . .' Masha intentionally did not call her step-mother 'Zhenya', which might have sounded false, and Grisha understood this.

'I've got an empty room, but they didn't want to stay with me,' smiled Masha, glad that her room really was free, and she herself likewise. 'Do you know, to be honest, I'm afraid to go alone. You weren't intending to go and see them today, by any chance?'

Twenty years earlier, when Masha, looking through the open-work fence at the blue bicycle, had cried, 'I want one like that!' she had sounded pig-headed. But now, amid the mourning and sorrow, she was so open and trusting that Tokarev recognized in her not only the former Masha Cholyshev but also the dream of her which he had nurtured for many years. It was not just her happy face that excited Tokarev, however, but also her tall and shapely body, which was itself undisguisedly drawn towards him.

Susanna Fyodorovna looked angrily at the youngsters, got up, and leaning on her stick, hobbled through to the coffin in the main hall. Neither Masha nor Tokarev paid any attention to her.

Everything about Masha, from her shoes, which no longer hurt, to her tousled brown curls, seemed to share the joy which shone in her green eyes: You see how marvellous it is! I've met you and I'm completely free. So what if I'm *here*: *you* are too, after all! I am keeping nothing from you, and feigning nothing. Otherwise I would be at the station just now, playing the loving step-daughter. But I am here, and I am glad to see you . . .

'So am I' Tokarev almost cried out.

When the speeches began and everyone went out into the main hall, Masha and Grishka went outside and climbed into one of the funeral buses, where they were later squeezed up against one another by the crowd. At the Novodevichy Convent cemetery they fell behind the other mourners and the police guard asked to see their passes.

'What is this? A picture house!' Masha laughed spitefully, and taking Grishka's hand, she led him away – past the convent wall, over the square, and into the lanes of the Medical Institute, where they started kissing passionately, ignoring both the twittering of the girl-students and the heart-rending barking of experimental dogs locked up in cages.

During the night Zhenya woke up feeling cold. Pashet was not beside her. She waited for about fifteen minutes, but Pashet did not come back. Throwing on her dressing-gown, she went through to the kitchen, and gasped at what she saw: Pashet was sitting on the windowsill.

'What are you doing?' She ran towards him.

'It's all right, I shan't fall out. Go to bed.'

'You'll catch cold. Let me bring a blanket.'

'Go to bed.'

On Sunday Zhenya was no longer typing out Tokarev's memoirs, and the old man spent the whole day drinking vodka, which he was strictly forbidden to do. At night he sat in the kitchen again, but did not open the window.

It would scarcely be possible to despise a woman more than Pashet despised Varvara Alekseyevna, Zhenya reflected. And yet he is grief-stricken. I had reckoned that her death would not upset him, and hurried to tell him about America. Poor Pashet. This is his second night without sleep, he is drinking, and thinking about God knows what. And tomorrow he'll be on his feet all day . . . For some reason the Tokarevs are taking the coffin to a church, although in my opinion it is indecent to take such a woman into a church. What about me? – she suddenly asked herself. Would it be decent for me? I'll get by without a religious funeral . . . Poor old Pashet. He's had no luck with his wives. But I did try. Oh, I was unfaithful to him whenever I could be – but another woman would have left him long ago. In Moscow he became unbearable. Why did I bother to bring him here? He felt warm and comfortable in Siberia, and he just ignored all those damned political questions.

He had me. He had to feed me, and above all, protect me from State Security. Pashet had no time to go into his differences with the Leviathan. And who did argue with the State in those days? We all held our tongues. We lived quietly, or rather, hid ourselves away. And if the day passed without your being arrested you just thanked your lucky stars . . .

Zhenya recalled how youthful, and even dashing, Pashet had been in those Siberian days, and how (admit it) she had been jealous of his female colleagues in the pit-design office. While she was studing at the Medical Institute, and later, when she stayed on to work there, it never entered her head to have an affair with another man. She used to race home at top speed, because everything in the town meant exile to her, and only their two-roomed flat was a little island of freedom. Zhenya hoped that they would be happy in Moscow too, but for Pashet it was evidently too late in life to get used to new people, surroundings and circumstances. This became apparent almost immediately, but the catastrophe struck six months later.

While waiting for the room which was firmly promised by the Coal Ministry, Zhenya and Pashet rented a tiny closet like a pencil-case, and almost every evening were visited by their new son-in-law – Grigory Yakovlevich Tokarev.

Once the conversation turned to the war, and Tokarev asked, drunkenly: 'I wonder what got into you, Pashet. You were an "internal émigré," an oppositionist – and suddenly you go and volunteer! It's out of character. It would have been much more logical for you to have stayed with the Germans. It's only one step from disaffection to collaboration . . .'

'Take him away,' said Cholyshev to his wife. He was not yet accustomed to hearing his son-in-law use the familiar form of address with him, and, in imitation of Zhenya, call him 'Pashet' instead of 'Pavel Rodionovich'. He made 'Pashet' sound like something you would call a puppy. Besides, the pencil-case was only partitioned off from the landlord's part of the flat with thin plywood.

Zhenya sat silently with her legs curled up on the corner of the settee, stroking Grishka's curly hair. She was angry with her husband. It seemed that their marriage, after eleven happy years, was unsuited to Moscow.

'You spent most of your life trembling . . . Oh, I'm sorry, Pashet . . .' Grishka faltered. 'But don't bury your head in the sand. Deep down, you're a brave fellow . . . Times are different now. It's all over with Stalinism.'

'And with Hungary too,' growled Cholyshev.

'Pashet, you're incurable . . .'

'They didn't manage to "cure" me: I was lucky . . .'

'And how were our glorious secret police supposed to get to you? You were sitting in a slit-trench!' Tokarev laughed.

'I certainly wasn't on the City Party Committee, that's true . . .'

'Pashet, stop it!' said Zhenya. 'Grishka didn't choose his father . . .'

'But I'm proud of my father!' protested Tokarev. 'He was an honest man.'

'All right, all right . . . But I'm not giving you any more to drink,' said Zhenya, placing the bottle beside her on the settee.

'You shouldn't be offended, Pashet,' said Tokarev. 'All I'm saying is that since you don't like Soviet power it would have been more logical for you to stay in occupied territory.'

'He's in occupied territory now,' said Zhenya with a sigh. 'He never goes outside in the evenings: it's as if there was a curfew. He just goes to and fro between this kennel and work.'

'At least I don't suck up to anybody. I don't go around shouting "Long live the romance of the virgin lands!" or "Glory to Leninist socialist legality!" ' said Cholyshev angrily, alluding to his son-in-law's latest articles. Tokarev was only just beginning to find his way into print, and he was not exactly discriminating.

'That's enough, Pashet,' his wife frowned. 'Do you really think that you are special and cannot adjust to Soviet power? Well, in the first place, it's not so . . . And secondly, what's the point? You really do sit in this den and never dare to venture out.

And who gains from that?'

'You,' said Cholyshev to himself.

'Nobody,' said Zhenya, raising her voice. 'And Grishka and Nadka . . .'

'Shh . . .' Now it was Tokarev's turn to take fright, although the landlord could scarcely have guessed who Nadya was and where she lived.

'Yes,' Zhenya went on fervent voice, 'Grishka and Nadka gave me shelter and saved me. He's like a brother to me . . .' She gave Tokarev a hug. 'And I'm determined to find Nadya, too. I will find her, you'll see. It's rotten of me not to have written to her for so many years. No, I don't intend to sit in a corner!'

She jumped up from the settee and stood before Cholyshev, looking stern and young, evidently quite prepared for any twist in her own fate and his.

'Don't imagine, Pashet, that you are so exceptional. Nothing of the sort. You're not an oppositionist or internal émigré. That was just flattery on Grisha's part. You're a perfectly ordinary mason.'

'What! Is he a freemason?' exclaimed Grisha, startled.

'If only he was . . .! Pashet's not a *free* mason; quite the opposite. I was thinking of that verse:

"... Stonemason, stonemason, in your white apron,
What are you building there, listen!"
"Hey, don't disturb us, we're busy at work,
We're building, we're building a prison." '

She declaimed the verse with feeling, but immediately felt embarrassed. 'My God, what clumsy poetry . . .' She felt uncomfortable and wanted to break off the argument. 'Forgive me, Pashet, but you are a mason. Of course, you are a very good man, a selfless man. It didn't even occur to you to hide from the war. You are very decent, very fair. You always put everything you had into your work. But it goes without saying that you, together with the whole Soviet people, have built . . . a prison.'

Tokarev was taken aback: 'Zheka, that's going too far . . .'

'And what alternative would you offer me?' Pavel flared up. With his grey hair and flushed cheeks he also looked young and determined, like an accused man listening to his sentence being read out. Zhenya understood that he would not retreat either.

'None. Absolutely nothing. I'm a mason myself. And always have been. Even in camp.'

'No, Zheka, no!' Tokarev protested. 'Don't speak so rashly. You're not guilty. And nor am I. I have never built any kind of prison, not even figuratively speaking.'

'Be quiet,' whispered Zhenya without turning round, and falling on her husband's shoulder, started crying.

'You're right, Pashet,' she said. 'You're right. There was nothing one could do. And there's still nothing now . . . My God, why did I start this conversation? I mean, there is no way out . . .'

But for himself Cholyshev found a way out, and a week later he took his pension. The Coal Ministry granted him early retirement.

I begged him on my knees, Zhenya remembered. I insisted that my pharmacology was no better – indeed, it was worse – than his coal pits. He would have none of it, wouldn't hear of it. He retired without even waiting for our firmly promised room. So we paid dearly for that moral act of renunciation . . . No, a man ought not to lock himself within four walls, like a housewife. Especially as he did not even have his own walls – only a couple of corners, where my jealous sovereign would wait and pine for me, while I looked for pretexts to come back late. Is it easy to put up with a fellow who has grown old before his time, and who, for want of anything better to do, settles scores with those who want to enjoy life? First and foremost, of course, with my friends! 'He's no use for such-and-such a reason . . . she's no use for some other reason . . .' I had only just managed to build up some human contacts, and he spoiled the pleasure of every friendship and meeting. I was starved of all this, and all he could say was: 'All your friends are time-servers.' Of course, Pashet was annoyed because I was now his one and only link with the outside world. I went out into life independently of him, and he simply could not come to terms with that. But let's face it, *I* didn't force him into his lair . . .

Deceiving her husband for the first time in the twelfth year of their marriage, Zhenya felt like a silly, helpless, forty-year-old idiot. She was embarrassed not only to undress in front of her lover, but even to take off her glasses.

So this is what life with the old grump has reduced me to, she thought, resentfully, but for some reason she immediately felt pulled back to Pashet, her former defence and support, and now quite simply the only being on Earth who prized her above all else . . . Yes, it was true, that jealous old squabbler held her dearer than anybody else – even that shrew Masha . . .

Ever since then Zhenya's longing to leave home had alternated with her gravitation towards home, and she was never at peace – constantly wanting to run off somewhere in order to return at once. Her life became restless, and much too bustling for her years, as though Zhenya Knysh was indeed running away from old age. She called herself a 'woman without a calling' – with no family, no children, and no work. For what kind of work does a Soviet person have? 'Service.' And he does that in low gear. So I waste the years on a cold war with my husband and on hot squabbles with myself. Nobody needs me, and there is nowhere for me to apply myself. My sympathy, my interest in people, my – if you like – willingness to take risks: it's all wasted . . . I have no personal life. Only a meagre, ragged, woman's biography. Lord, if only Pashet was more trusting of others, how much easier life would be! Or if he was hopelessly ill, if one had to win him back from death daily . . . But my misanthrope requires no great exploits of me. No, if I returned from the lab on time, I would throw myself out of the window one evening . . . As it is, I'm normally only two or three hours late, but at least I fly home at breakneck speed. Yes, Pashet is my home. Cramped, dull, awful – but he's still home. I have never had any other . . . And yet, it would have been more honest to leave altogether. Or at least come clean with him about everything. Because the reason he's so jealous and worried is that he believes I've never had an affair – but that I *could* have one any day now! If I confessed, he would suffer terribly, but then calm down. His jealousy is his uncertainty about my 'tomorrow', because all my 'yesterdays' are beyond suspicion . . . And he's quite right. It's all nonsense. A timid search for a kindred soul. Pitiful attempts to get a rest from Pashet. Intimacy was never the aim in all this. It was because I was too shy to ask the procuress for the key . . .

'The procuress' was Zhenya's nickname for an old friend of her camp days, no longer young, but energetic and doggedly self-willed. Within a week of being rehabilitated, this intrepid woman managed to land herself a self-contained flat, and willingly – indeed insistently – took care of her junior comrade. But the 'procuress' was nosy, and as a price for letting Zhenya into her room she tried to delve into corners of Zhenya's soul which Zhenya herself preferred not to explore.

Fleeting encounters in cafés and cinemas, even in the institute library – unhurried, with semi-tones predominant; calm relationships which need not end in anything – in short, all the great joys of student life which Zhenya was done out of by camp and exile, enticed her more than the complicated, often intense and heavy, physical affairs.

. . . But now, thank God, all my attempts to escape are over . . . I was so scared that my step-daughter would catch me. For some reason it was precisely Masha I was afraid of. I suppose it was because she knew half of Moscow and turned up in the most unexpected places. And of course, she would have split on me to Pavel without a second thought. But now I can sleep peacefully. I'm too old . . . But I'm running away, just the same. I've got my sights set on America: that's also running away. But it's only for a couple of months, three at the most . . . Do I have that long? And how shall I leave Pashet? He'll go to seed with no one to look after him. Is America really more important than him? Or have I actually made up my mind to leave him? Never! I must take that bottle away from him. Tomorrow will be a hard day. I hope I can persuade Pashet to go straight to the cemetery without looking in at the church . . .

It was drizzling. The coffin was carried for as far as was possible on a cart, and mud from the wheels spattered the mourners. The old man was angry because Zhenya had insisted on accompanying him, and looking tired and aged, was picking her way over the sticky ground in high heels. This irritated him and distracted his mind from his dead wife.

For two days Cholyshev had been thinking unceasingly about Bronka, not so much forgiving her as blaming himself. And now, hurrying behind the cart, he was impatient for them to stop and open the coffin. As if Bronka's dead face could explain something . . .

On Saturday, after reading the memoirs, he had been afraid to go behind the screen, but now he was in such a hurry to look at the dead woman's face that the cemetery seemed endless. The crematorium would have been better . . . Although there was more space in the open. Soon he and Bronka would be face to face (it did not matter that her eyes were closed) and then all these people who were around would disturb him no more than the drizzle, or the trees still standing in the distance, or the excavator digging a grave . . .

It became soggy underfoot and the coffin had to be carried the rest of the way. Pavel did not offer his shoulder, though, but continued to shuffle behind, with Zhenya clinging to his elbow.

(. . . A month before, during the operation, Cholyshev had felt sorry for Bronka as he waited for news, and almost prayed for her not to regain consciousness. Why operate if there was no hope? They could give her opium, and let her be . . . But Masha and her brother, the hefty railwayman, believed their mother would be saved, and, doped with sedatives, sat with their arms around each other on a white hospital bench.

Cholyshev's son-in-law mooned about in the vestibule, often

going out to smoke, then returning and slouching against a wall with his eyes for some reason trained on the registry window. The old man, who was concentrating on death, paid scant attention to Tokarev.

All the possible options end in death, he was thinking. If Bronka pulls through, but ends up bedridden, she still won't escape death. So it would be better if she died now, without the suffering . . . It would be better for Masha, too, and for that noodle Viktor. If their mother has to lie in a ward with fourteen others, all of them on death row, she'd be better off dead. Whatever way you look at it, death is the best outcome. But it's not for me to decide, and Bronka is under anaesthetic. Life has an infinite number of possibilities, but death has only one, like the summit of a mountain. It's a blind alley, but at the same time a culmination. If you look back down from the point of death, you see the whole of Bronka's life and suddenly unravel its meaning . . . Why is Grishka staring at that window? Ah, he's playing at 'combinations', seeing how many words he can form from 'REGISTRATION'. 'Stares'? No, there's only one 's'. 'Stair'. 'Treat' . . .)

That was what he had thought when they were operating on Varvara Alekseyevna, and feeling no link between himself and her, he wished she would die quickly and painlessly. But now, as he trudged through the graveyard mud, he felt as if he were not dragging himself after the coffin, but the coffin was pulling him along. It was as if the coffin (which, thank God, was not draped with red cloth) contained one half of Cholyshev, and the other half was obediently trailing along behind the first. And he could not wait to reach the grave, where the young men would remove from their shoulders the heavy, damp, roughly-made box.

The rain mixed with his tears, and when they stopped the old man could not see Bronka's face. It was as if he had suddenly fainted, and Bronka was not lying in the coffin but was floating in front of him, at all ages – from a two-year-old girl to an elderly woman. And he wished only one thing: that Bronka was alive, and would always be alive, because her death turned out to be not the end of Bronka, but the last line in a sentence passed on Cholyshev in this unfenced, desolate, country graveyard.

He wept silently, in bursts, shrugging off Zhenya's arm, and still he could not see the dead woman. When it was his turn to press his lips to Bronka's forehead, he could not make out her face through the rain.

The coffin-lid was hammered down, and it brought no relief. The old man burned with sorrow inside, and outside he was chilled, as though by a draught, by a consciousness of guilt and orphanhood, just like sixty years before, when his father was buried, and a year later when the refugee was strangled, and later still, when he could not find his mother . . . Guilt and orphanhood were inseparable, because orphanhood was retribution for his guilt, although he did not drown his father in the river or strangle the refugee. But he did cause grief to his mother, Lyubov Simonovna, by turning away from her in the difficult years, by giving her neither filial love nor simple human sympathy, and finally by outraging her with his absurd relationship with Leokadia . . .

As far as Bronka was concerned, Cholyshev ruined her for no reason at all, palmed her off on to that scum Drozd, and quashed all the rudiments of goodness in her. They must have existed in her, after all! From then on things took their course . . . No one understands the nature of cancer. Perhaps it is not a disease, but a combination of inconsolable grief and unalleviated injuries . . . Perhaps the young Bronka expected boundless love from him, and he humiliated her with condescending pity and pointless respectability. And now, forty-odd years later, all the wrongs, humiliations and sadness had germinated to produce a tumour, and dragged Varvara Alekseyevna to her grave . . .

Cholyshev watched the sticky mound of earth rise towards the rain, and felt with horror his hopeless loneliness, although Zhenya was holding his hand and Masha and her husband were standing nearby.

The funeral feast overwhelmed the old man. There were about sixty people crammed into the two rooms – his daughter's and her neighbour's. There were not enough chairs; almost all the guests had to stand.

Not even a third of them turned up at the cemetery, thought Cholyshev. Nor at the church service.

He was worried by that church service. To the deceased, of course, even though she was a member of the Communist Party, it made no difference. But it could land Masha in the soup, even thought she was not a Party member, since she worked in an ideological department.

Amidst the hubbub of the funeral the old man suddenly felt like being nice to his daughter, but she was standing at the other end of the room. Around her, guests were eating and drinking greedily, although the fare was pretty miserable: the usual drinks, tinned sprats, bottled Hungarian salads, and the old potatoes with too little butter. The Tokarevs had not been over-generous with their funeral feast – but then, they never had any money. What would happen if they found out about the church service at Masha's institute?

Masha was getting visibly drunk, and it was not worth his making his way through the crowd to her with his paternal affection and all-forgivingness. Just as on Saturday, they would not have succeeded in sharing their grief together. And nobody else was grieving. For Grisha, for Viktor the fool (who would be getting Bronka's country cottage!) and for her granddaughter Svetlana (who was in the Crimea and was not even sent for), Varvara Alekseyevna's death was no loss.

Masha was becoming more and more obviously tipsy. Her shrill, nasty laughter spilled over into tears more and more often, and the old man plunged deeper into his feelings of hopelessness. Zhenya, conscious that Pashet was in no mood for her, remained by the door, and it was from there, through the din of the gathering, that Cholyshev now heard: 'My girl, apply at once! Without any question whatsoever. Apply tomorrow! You'll see:

they'll let you out within the month!'

Old Cholyshev gave a shudder as he caught sight of the speaker, a fat, whiskered woman. 'I was prepared for anyone, but I didn't expect to meet that brazen Amazon at Bronka's funeral feast,' he thought. But looking round, he counted several more of Zhenya's friends in the room.

Grishka must have invited them; he has everything in common with . . . *her*. In his annoyance the old man could not bring himself to say his wife's name.

'You must go, darling! Have an affair with some interesting American. Women look a fraction of their age in the States. Your fif-, I'm sorry, dear, I'm sorry . . . your forty years will instantly be reduced to twenty-nine!' the Amazon gushed joyfully.

Cholyshev was not keen on any of Zhenya's friends, but this one annoyed him more than all the others put together. Every sentiment she expressed infuriated him, but he had never once dared to contradict her. That was because he suffered from a complex, never having been in prison.

What do I know about convicts? he reproached himself. I hardly ever went to the mines, so as not to come into contact with them. I was ashamed of being free. I didn't know I was also a forced labourer. Not a convict, of course, but an 'unfree' mason . . .

'Have the courage to apply!' the Amazon gushed on. 'And if they turn you down, dear, write to Mr Brezhnev – or even better, to Mr Andropov. It's more in his department's line. They refused to give me a visa to go to Paris once, but after a letter to the KGB they even apologized for the delay.'

'Give your advice to someone else,' said Tokarev. 'Zheka will never write to the *okhranka*.'*

'Grisha, please . . .'

'Listen,' Tokarev repeated, 'we all deeply respect your past. But Zheka, by the way, was also in the camps, and – I'm telling you in plain Russian – she will never write to the *okhranka*.'

* The *okhranka* was the secret police department in pre-revolutionary Russia. [Tr.]

118

What are they jabbering about? thought Cholyshev. You'd think they were in the Visas Office.

It suddenly occurred to him that if Varvara Alekseyevna had lived, or rather, gone on dying for ever, Zhenya would not have made up her mind to go to America. His throat tightened at the thought of this, and he wished he could escape from the smoky room, at least into the little park outside. But it was a funeral feast, after all.

I wonder where that hairy chap is? thought the old man, remembering the bearded fellow who had offered to ease his mind on Saturday. Of course, he was just blethering, but at least it would make a change from this exit-visa business.

Right at the start of the feast Cholyshev had seen him near the district nurse – a rather plain, swarthy girl – who had tended the dying woman all last week. But the crowd around the table had gradually dispersed. Many of the guests, including Zhenya, had left the room, and those who remained were deep in an argument, which Cholyshev could not follow, about reincarnation. The bearded man was not among them.

In the corridor, which was also packed with guests, the middle-aged Amazon was praising Moscow's Taganka Theatre to the skies.

'No, no, I'm not at all conservative. In my other life, I mean, before my arrest, I adored the Moscow Art Theatre and worshipped the Maly. At that time I needed a curtain. It gave me joy to see living people on the stage. You say there aren't living people at the Taganka? I don't mind! Times change, and I don't want to go back to Ostrovsky's Zamoskvorechie.'*

No, it's America you want to go to, thought Cholyshev, but then remembered that it was Zhenya, not the Amazon, who wanted to go to America.

* The Taganka Theatre is Moscow's most experimental, avant-garde theatre. The realist dramatist, Alexander Ostrovsky (1823–86) is one of the classic writers of the Russian stage. Many of his plays, some of them set in the Zamoskvorechie district of Moscow, were performed at the Maly Theatre. [Tr.]

He walked all round the cluttered communal flat once more. The bearded man was in neither of the rooms, and in the kitchen Zhenya and Grisha were sitting with some of their women-friends, including the ubiquitous Amazon-procuress, who contrived to turn up in all corners of the flat at once.

I suppose she's expatiating on how progressive and up-to-date she is, thought the old man crossly. Oh, I dare say I'd have changed my tune if they had taken away eighteen years of my life . . . They took away more than seventy years of my life . . .

His argument with himself was interrupted by the 'procuress': 'I'm surprised at you, Grishka,' she was booming. 'A handsome young fellow like you – and you're practically drawing your pension. You've run away: "Don't bother me! It's not my problem!" – That's your attitude! But you're a writer! You're obliged to be at the centre of humanity, at the centre of all that's going on. But where are you? I open our best literary journal, and what do I find? No Tokarev. I pick up the *Literary Gazette* – again, no Tokarev.'

She's getting her own back on him for calling the KGB the *okhranka*, Cholyshev decided.

'New stories and novels are coming out all the time, incredibly important discussions are started, a whole mass of burning questions has accumulated – and you, Grishenka, say nothing, and we can't understand what's going on without your wise explanations.'

'Come off it, that's enough,' frowned Tokarev.

'No, my dear, you can't brush aside your grateful readers that easily. You can't beckon us and enlighten us, and then just drop us when it suits you. It's not right. It's not nice. We were proud of you, we trusted you. And now rumour has it that you've succumbed to the new – or rather, the old – trend, and started believing in God . . . In other words, you've run off to your ivory tower and don't even want to think about us.'

'Leave him alone,' said Zhenya softly.

'You're always mollycoddling him,' smiled the Amazon. 'But

he's not a child, he's a teacher of life. God's all very well, Grisha, but don't be a simpleton. You've given in, you've faded. I'm afraid you're imitating your father-in-law. That's his *idée fixe*: not to get involved, not to participate in anything. Pashet – the apostle of the moral underground . . .'

'Oh no you don't! Leave me out of this,' muttered the old man. He was dispirited. He had never shared his thoughts with the procuress. Was Zhenya so frank with her? Besides, on this old woman's lips, 'Pashet' sounded as if it had a small 'P': like the title of a profession, not a name.

'Leave him,' said Zhenya again. 'It's impossible to work as a critic these days. That's why he left it.'

'What did he leave it for?' exclaimed the Amazon. 'The Church? His private life? Philistinism?'

'Now, listen,' Tokarev frowned. 'Don't you think these questions are a little offensive?'

'But I am offensive – had you forgotten? I'm a dreadful old bird, you know – I lived with the roster-guards in camp . . . You can accuse me of any sin you can think of, but I still love you, my prickly one. I hate to see you robbing yourself. It's bad enough that Soviet power . . .' (The procuress did lower her voice here.) '. . . that Soviet power has short-changed us, without our restricting ourselves into the bargain! What kind of nonsense is that? Life is short, girls and boys. Take my word for it, as an unhappy old woman. All my pleasures disappeared long ago. No roster-guards are going to sleep with me now!' She winked at Zhenya, and Zhenya blushed.

She told everyone else about this old shrew, thought Cholyshev, but she never shared anything with me . . . I scared her with my squeamishness.

'So I just get on with my business. I can look after myself, because I may be an old woman, but I'm not a stupid, faint-hearted chicken. But you, Grisha, are a chicken. You used to love appearing in print! Hold on, hold on, Zhenya, I know what you want to say: that you can't get any enlightened thoughts into print nowadays, that the censors have clamped down, and so on and so forth. I know, I agree! So what do we do? Sit and wait for the fog to clear? And if it doesn't clear? What if it's like this for ever? Or gets even worse? The Chinese are coming, they say. What will we do then? Commit *hara-kiri*?'

'Oh, come on, don't frighten us at this time of night!' said Tokarev with an ironic grin.

'I'm not trying to frighten you. I'm speaking sense. If you're brave enough, fight! Look at Academician Sakharov – he's organized a Human Rights Committee. I bow down to him, I respect him, although I don't believe any good will come of it. Open resistance – alas – is useless. Even in the camps I knew that. It's stupid to rebel; adapting oneself is much more sensible. It's the time-servers, not the rebels, who improve the world and make it more bearable to live in. My father, bless his soul, was an old Social Democrat,* and what did he achieve? He got himself shot, and I got ten years in camp and another eight in exile. Of course, Father was a Jew – a rebel by nature, in other words. But even for a Jew it wasn't worth rebelling.'

'If you're born to crawl, you'll never fly,' sighed her friend Zhenya.

'And what about your storm petrel† – didn't he crawl? Kicked up a bit of a fuss at first, but when the Romanov dynasty was three hundred years old he came back to the fold as meek as a lamb. Why? Because he wanted a decent life. He attacked the Bolsheviks too to begin with. Wrote his *Unseasonable Thoughts*. Then he was imprisoned. He signed various petitions, and even fled the country. Then, when the dollars ran out, he came crawling back and even started hissing about "bringing the enemy to their knees"

* A member of the party which split into Bolsheviks and Mensheviks in 1903. [Tr.]
† The writer Maxim Gorky, whose 'Song of the Storm Petrel' (1901), a 'prose poem', glorified the petrel as the herald of a storm – clearly intended as a symbol of revolution. His earlier 'Song of the Falcon' (1895) compared the falcon, who has known the joy and freedom of flight, with the snake, who is 'born to crawl, and will never fly'. [Tr.]

. . . And so to this day literary critics haven't been able to decide whether he was a falcon or a –'

'An unfortunate Russian intellectual,' said Zhenya.

'Save your pity for that Tokarev of yours, my girl. Explain to him that however you look at it, his life in this world will come to an end, and there won't be another one. You caught a glimpse of the "afterlife" in camp. Tell him there's nothing there. Tell him not to rely too much on God. It's *here* that you're needed, Grisha, but you've built yourself some kind of monk's cell.'

'Look, why are you plaguing me like this?' Grisha shouted. 'I'm not in any monk's cell. You want to know if I am writing? Yes, I am writing. I'm writing for my own desk drawer. Do you understand that?'

'Well, that's silly,' said the shrew calmly. 'You should be writing for us, who are alive today, not for your "desk", not for the future. Tomorrow's geniuses will write for future generations: they'll know better what to write about. Anyway, I don't understand what has happened – was there no censorship before? As far as I know, *we* are the same as before, living in the same country where the year before last this very G. Tokarev reasoned with us from the pages of a world-famous journal. All right, let's say the country has got worse, or if you like, we ourselves have gone downhill. In that case let G. Tokarev condescend to his suffering readers and spread good and eternal thoughts, but of a lower quality. You have to think of your readers first, not of your pride. I dare say your only consideration is that you mustn't "stain" yourself . . .'

'Shut up. I'm sick of your cynicism.'

'That's not cynicism, Grishka. It's worldly wisdom,' smiled the procuress. 'But writing for your desk is perhaps not cynicism, but – excuse me – masturbation . . . Is that what you are going to do while waiting for the perfect lady – in other words, a perfect age – to come along? What if she never turns up? You're young: you need fame. No, Grisha, we're not going to let you go to waste – are we, Pavel Rodionovich?'

'I told you to leave me in peace!' Cholyshev turned away and suddenly saw the bathroom door bursting open and the plain nurse diving out with a depressed and shameful face, followed by the bearded guest, looking not at all kindly, but rather sly and merry.

'So there you are, Pavel Rodionovich! I've been looking for you. I was hoping we could have a chat. Still, it's not the last time we'll see each other: there will be other times to chat!' The long-haired guest smiled and clapped Cholyshev on the back. Then he nodded to the nurse – 'Off you go, kid!' – and squeezed past Cholyshev into the kitchen.

'You're here, old man?' he said to Grisha. 'What's the argument about?'

'I'm scolding your friend for turning away from life,' laughed the Amazon. 'You see, he's imitating his father-in-law. But what is permissible for Jupiter, in our case an elderly man . . .' She winked at the bearded man, who was young enough to be her grandson, as though they were the same age.

'Undoubtedly so,' he replied, assuming a dignified air and trying to look twice as old and four times as drunk. 'Don't you argue, old chap . . .' He raised his hand, anticipating Tokarev's objection. 'And you, Pavel Rodionovich,' he turned to Cholyshev, 'are wrong again. I explained to you on Saturday: there's no need to be afraid of death. Nor of life, either. Life, you see, is –'

'Exactly, exactly!' the shrew chimed in. 'How marvellous that you also think so! You see, Grishenka, your friend and I have scarcely met, but we're in total agreement. No, it's stupid, stupid, to shun real life. Nothing exists apart from it –'

'One moment, with respect. May I –' The long-maned fellow raised both hands.

'No, no, I've started so I'll finish,' the woman hurried on. 'I'm glad that you and I are of the same opinion. Without you, everyone kept interrupting me.'

'And quite rightly . . . Who told you, my dear, that life ends here on Earth? Science has established that the soul does not die. In the United States they bring up to a hundred people back to life every month. Up to a *hundred*, do you hear? Every month a hundred souls depart this life, and they are brought back again by force, against their will. They want to leave, but the resuscitators won't let them. Human souls strive towards the other world. They see their parents and relatives there, they want to be with them, and leave them only when their mother or father tells them: "Go back!" And even then the return to us is a torment to them. And you say: "Life ends here!" '

'What rubbish!' said the Amazon with a smirk.

'No, my dear. It's not rubbish at all. Death is not the end, but merely a passage to another, higher state. And in fact, our life here isn't really life as such, but a rough copy, a rehearsal. And at the same time it is a test – a sort of examination to select those worthy of the better world.'

'Listen, son, don't give me that crap. You're reeking of vodka and women. Don't expect me to believe that you alternate those joys with incense and boring thoughts about Heaven. You might fool the others, but not me . . .' The Amazon shook with aggrieved laughter and left the kitchen.

I could listen to Masha if I wanted to know about reincarnation, thought Cholyshev. The bearded fellow no longer amused him, and the whiskered procuress annoyed him even more than the former did, because she stirred up his simmering jealousy of his wife.

How come she christened me a mason – he thought of his wife – but forgives that shrew everything? *She* is allowed to adapt to Soviet power and live life to the full; but I'm not allowed even a little latitude. The former mason has to tremble in his co-operative den, waiting for his wife to deign to appear. But that mason could also go to work in an office, by the way . . . The old man forgot that it was Zhenya who had tried to persuade him not to retire, and that now, being over seventy, he would have had to stay at home in any case. But, while forgetting his age, Cholyshev remembered about America, and felt worse than ever. He wandered into Masha's room, but Masha was too busy gossiping with the shrew to be bothered with her father.

The procuress, wounded by the argument in the kitchen, declared to Masha that she deemed the funeral service extremely odd since Varvara Alekseyevna had not been a believer. Masha angrily replied that, on the contrary, her mother had been deeply religious. The Amazon countered that as a clever woman and a hedonist, Varvara Alekseyevna must have scorned the idea of another world.

Just then Tokarev came into the room but he did not try to restrain his wife. He was extremely angry with the procuress. Not that it would have been easy to restrain Masha.

'You're as ignorant as a felt boot!' she was bawling. 'What have you got in your stupid head apart from baubles and beads? You're like mutton dressed as lamb – it's disgusting to look at you . . . Faith! Do you know what "believing" means? Do you think it means palming off a dress from Tbilisi on your mother and letting her believe it's from Paris? You're so used to fooling people, you think faith is also deception, eh? Well, just get the hell out of here. I don't know what my husband was thinking of, inviting scum like you into a Christian house.'

The Amazon, normally so boisterous and self-confident, dumbly flapped her bare eyelids and started to wheeze and shrink like a burst air-mattress. But suddenly she dived out of the room as though she had been stung and, encountering Zhenya at the door, she burst into tears on her shoulder.

'What's happened?' Zhenya asked her husband.

'I . . . I didn't understand . . .' Cholyshev faltered.

'What do you mean, Pashet?'

Zhenya intentionally did not notice her step-daughter and Tokarev. She could not reproach Grisha in front of Masha. The old man stood spellbound, gazing at his blushing wife as though she had just appeared before him for the first time, and his amazement would have gone on even longer, had not Masha started up again: 'What are you shouting the odds about, Zhenya? And why pick on Father? He wouldn't hurt a fly. It was me who chased her out. No, I'm not drunk – I'm soberer than you. Go and run away to the States and get yourself some nice clothes. You don't love Russia anyway, that's what I say!' screamed Masha, as though Zhenya was planning to emigrate to America. 'Go and leave! You're not Russian at all. Grisha and I are Russians: we were born here and we'll die here – we'll never leave. But you can go to hell. Take her away, Dad, or I won't be responsible for my actions.'

'Masha!' Tokarev intervened at last, but just as on Saturday, far too late. Pashet and Zhenya were already hurrying down the stairs.

And so the old man was left on his own. Now Zhenya returned early from the laboratory, cooked in the kitchen, and read in the living-room (at least she did not type), but it was as if she did not even notice her husband. They scarcely exchanged words. Zhenya did not want to discuss her trip for fear that Pashet would make her feel sorry for him and dissuade her.

Pashet just suffered in silence: To hell with America: it doesn't matter. But going to see Nadya . . . that means turning the clock back, to 1945, to that fork in Zhenya's life. She thinks she miscalculated by waiting for me, and now she wants to go and see what she missed out on. It's obvious: I am old – she's miserable with me. And America is compensation for those long boring years of being worn down by a bad-tempered old squabbler . . .

The couple were quiet, but the flat became noisy. Overcoming Zhenya's resistance, the Amazon became a more and more frequent visitor, together with her female friends whom Pashet found so hard to understand. Their voices merged into an intolerable buzz, from which the old man with difficulty picked out the words: 'Visa Office . . . United States . . . Invitation . . . They'll let you go . . . They'll refuse . . .' He had never suspected that so many people were in love with foreign countries and had nothing better to do than to busy themselves with getting out, as though life in Russia weren't life at all, but penal servitude. The appearance of these dolled-up beauties immediately turned the room into a beggarly hovel. Spreading out their denim skirts and jangling their bracelets, the ladies vied with each other in cursing the leadership for being so ungenerous with exit visas.

Their husbands probably denounce the regime, and these women are just parroting their husbands' opinions, Cholyshev scowled. Their husbands are no dissidents: they're just lazy, indiscreet menials, covetous of the master's way of life. Landless peasants. They're worse than serfs: at least they ploughed the land. But these people grovel and yelp because not enough clothes and food and trips abroad are handed out to them . . . They're like some kind of special order – not an order of knights, or monks, but the Party's chosen few. They're no good at anything, and nobody apart from the present wretched authorities would keep them. I was afraid of Soviet power, and worked even harder than was required of me, just to buy myself a few hours of peace. But this lot aren't afraid of a thing, and screw all they can out of old Sofia Vlasievna* . . .

The denim ladies, like clockwork dolls, kept repeating: 'No, no, don't apply together. They won't let you both go!'

So I'm a kind of hostage, thought the old man gloomily.

Zhenya meanwhile collected the necessary documents.

'Don't sulk, Pashet.' She would, none the less, occasionally press herself close to her husband. 'I'm not leaving for ever. I'm sure I shan't be able to stand it for long over there. Everything is different with them, and they themselves will be different after all this time. Alf doesn't limp any more, and Nadya has her daughters.'

Cholyshev took this as a hint that if Zhenya had taken the chance to leave she would have had children.

'You won't have time to miss me before I'm back. I know you don't like this bustle all around. These women are impossible: one of them wants me to take something out for her, another wants me to bring something back. They're all so full of advice . . .'

'Oh, I've come to terms with that. But I don't see much

* 'Rhyming slang' for *Sovetskaya vlast'* (Soviet power). [Tr.]

128

of you behind all these females.'

'When I get back I'll be with you all the time . . .'

'When you get back I'll hear nothing but: "Ah, Long Beach!" and "Oh, Pasadena!" And you'll feel as miserable in Russia as a soldier in barracks. You'll start all over again, trying to get to the West.'

'I shan't go then . . .' Zhenya sighed, startled by the depth of his sadness. 'I've lost the inclination . . . To be honest, I shall be glad if they turn down my application.'

But fate never pampered Cholyshev, and Zhenya Knysh was given a passport for foreign travel without any difficulty.

In the last week the bustle reached a peak. Zhenya slept no more than two hours a night and ran about from shops to friends, going crazy from lack of sleep, instructions and requests.

'I'll rest in the plane,' she tried to cheer herself, hugging her husband. 'Pashet, why don't you say anything, silly? You'll make me howl! It's not for the rest of my life, you know . . . Let me go just for a month. Surely you can stand one month?'

'It's not me I'm thinking about . . . But if things are hectic here, in America it will be twice as bad. You'll go charging round like a mad thing, determined not to miss anything, examining one thing after another – and you'll collapse from the pace and from all the new impressions . . .'

In the enormous faceless glass hall of Sheremetyevo Airport the women who had turned out to see Zhenya off sighed: 'It's all changed.'

'This partition wasn't here.'

'Neither was this one.'

Pavel could not understand how something so lifeless could possibly change. They wipe the floor after you with a cloth, and it's as if you had never been there. Like in Heaven – no traces . . .

But in Heaven, he thought, there's no customs.

No one paid any attention to the old man. His wife and son-in-law were surrounded. And Zhenya and Grisha took so long to say goodbye that Cholyshev wondered if his wife had not decided on the trip for the sole purpose of being able to cling like that to Grisha with impunity in full view of everyone.

But then Zhenya, after hastily kissing her women-friends, embraced her husband.

'Pashet, forgive me . . . When I come back it will all be different . . . '

But the dispirited old man gave no heed to her sobs and merely waited patiently for his wife to be called behind the blue and yellow plastic partition.

Right up to the last minute Cholyshev still could not believe she would go. But Zhenya soared up into the air, and Cholyshev, turning down a lift in somebody's car, shuffled off to the bus stop.

The day was autumnally spacious. Bouncing on the seat of the empty bus, the old man reflected: It's a good thing that I am in Moscow. In what other town can one lose oneself so easily? In Siberia or the Ukraine you'd be plagued with neighbours.

He looked out of the window with curiosity, however, realizing that he was now presented with a mass of free time. If he felt like it he could go out of town, or go for a stroll in a park. Perhaps he would while away half a day playing chess in a boulevard with similar sickly old men. What a pity that the warm days were coming to an end, and he had long forgotten the most complicated gambits. Ah, if only he had had such freedom fifty years earlier . . .

Having been excessively cautious in his youth, he now had the urge to do something outrageous. But all that came into his head was . . . cinemas.

On the first day he sat through three films in a row – one Arabic, one Indian, and one Yugoslavian. The next morning, without even taking his coffee, he set off to the centre to see a new Italian film, but it proved to be no better than the previous day's. The cinema developed into a kind of daytime soporific for the old man. Masha and Grisha would have split their sides laughing if they had known *what* he was watching. But in a dark and empty auditorium, solitude merely matched solitude. Modern Asian cinematography could not disappoint, for it promised nothing. The only thing that hurt was an occasional awareness that over in the States Zhenya was watching first-class films, while he was amusing himself with this . . .

Pavel would return home in an anxious mood, eat something straight from the fridge, and then be at a loose end until late evening. Although a call from New York would cost many dollars, and Alf, by all accounts, was tight-fisted, Cholyshev still hoped that Zhenya would telephone. Given the time-difference, that could happen any time from late afternoon until morning. Cholyshev did not wish to be the first to telephone.

For six days the telephone was silent, and on the seventh day Masha, Grisha, and even their sixteen-year-old daughter Svetlana arrived in a great hurry.

'There's bad news, Dad . . .' said Masha, puffing as though she had run to the seventh floor instead of taking the lift. She thrust into his hands a rough yellow form on which strange Latin letters seemed to jump about: the old man tried to read them – JENJA TJAJELO BOLNA – 'Jenja is seriously ill' – but the letters refused to sit together, and even when they did they meant little to him, because 'Jenja' certainly was not the Zhenya who lived in this room, who, it seemed, had not flown across the ocean but just popped out quickly to see a friend. The room still preserved the tidiness left by Zhenya. Everything in it brought her to mind, because the tidiness *was* Zhenya. How could a worthless scrap of yellow paper change anything in the room, or in Cholyshev himself?

'Dad, don't worry . . . Lie down . . . It's probably not so serious as it sounds. But you lie down . . .' Masha gabbled, and the son-in-law and granddaughter looked past the old man.

'Go away. I want to be alone,' said Cholyshev hoarsely.

But just then the telephone rang and Grisha grabbed the receiver, nervously motioning to the others to keep quiet. His Adam's apple twitched: 'Nadya! Nadka! Yes, yes . . . I hear you . . .

Yes . . .' And unable to control himself, he broke down and wept.

'Daddy . . .' Svetlana started sobbing in unison with her father.

'Dad . . .' Masha was last to start crying. She held her father firmly to prevent him from grabbing the receiver from Grisha.

None the less he heard Nadya's voice, changed by time, distance and an American accent – 'Pavel Rodionovich . . .' – but then another (calm) female voice said something in English and the line went quiet.

Masha collected herself first. She produced from her shabby shopping bag a blood-pressure gauge and wrapped the black cuff tightly around her father's arm.

'I'm all right, I'm all right . . .' Cholyshev tried to push her away.

What was the point of taking his blood pressure? *Zhenya* no longer existed – and not just in this room, but anywhere, even the United States. But surely this could not be *it* – despite the telegram and the strange long ringing of the telephone and Nadya's howling across the ocean. *It* doesn't happen that way. Look at how Bronka suffered: that was *it* . . . Or when his father drowned, there was the river, and the sealed-up coffin . . . Or his mother: he never found her, but there was the morgue and piles of corpses. And during the war he could have touched dead bodies with his hands. All of those were *deaths*. But Zhenya – living Zhenya, whom he loved and tormented, whom he forgave nothing, from whom he had parted without making it up to her . . . how could *it* have happened to Zhenya? Would she no longer be with Cholyshev, but with all those others who had long since departed?

Suddenly it sank in that he would never see his wife again, and the old man shouted: 'Go away, all of you! Get out of here!'

But Masha was squeezing the rubber tube, saying: 'Dad, keep still.' And suddenly she whispered to her husband: 'Phone for an ambulance.'

And so it was that Pavel Cholyshev found himself in one of six beds in a hospital ward. His was beside the window. It was still warm outside.

Cholyshev was not the most hopeless case, merely old and unhappy. Old age and grief are no reason to undergo heart treatment. But that evening he had simply not had the strength to argue with his daughter.

'Look, I can't be with all of you at once,' Masha had shouted angrily. 'Who will look after you? In hospital you'll be cared for . . .'

Pavel wanted only one thing: to float away on his divan-bed as if it were a raft, and slowly – like a slow-motion replay – to pass a movie of Zhenya through his memory, right from the beginning. He could not explain to the Tokarevs that he was not afraid of death. An empty flat was much more terrible. But even the flat was not empty yet, as the old man filled it with Zhenya: Zhenya in all times and perspectives and dresses.

His daughter and son-in-law were scared to leave him, helpless and uncared-for, with his blood pressure up, and had him brought by ambulance to this ward, where it was harder to remember his wife, but easier at least to prepare for his own death. Two patients had just been wheeled out of the ward to intensive care, and this event gave rise at first to jokes and at night to insomnia in the ward.

Cholyshev could not sleep, either, though he was indifferent even to the pain in his chest – the first symptom of a heart attack. He was worried by something else. They had not talked it all out, they had not resolved anything, they had left all the bad feeling for when she came back . . .

He kept imagining that Zhenya was alive, as though their quarrel had crossed out her death. And because he believed in this, yet knew in his heart that she was dead, he had no peace, his blood pressure did not fall, and the pain remained hot and sharp like a skewer.

So what if I die? he tried to console himself, but began to regret that he did not believe in Heaven or a future life and would therefore not see Zhenya again. He had not accompanied her to the grave, had not kissed her, had not thrown earth on to the coffin

. . . Or had she been cremated? Those Americans hadn't written a word. They understood that they had ruined Zhenya . . .

Time almost stood still in the ward. The patients quarrelled lazily or bantered mirthlessly with one another. Their jokes did not touch the old man. He thought unceasingly about his wife's death. His thoughts wore him out, but held him here, on this side of death, on a hospital bed with its head raised.

'Why? What for? Who is to blame?' The questions flashed in his brain with the insistence of a traffic-light. Was it the angina? The strain of a long flight? The excitement of meeting Nadya? But people with angina pectoris live, fly to America . . . and what kind of excitement could there be, if Nadya and Zhenya were friends for only a year and a half, and that was thirty years ago? Or was Zhenya's death retribution? Was it that by not leaving in 1945 she had betrayed her stars, and now, when she changed her mind, it was too late? But if Zhenya's destiny was in America, it means her years with me were a mistake. All twenty-eight years – for nothing? All right, in Moscow we exasperated each other. I was jealous of everyone she knew and tormented her. But in Siberia she had seemed to be happy . . .

'In Siberia she had no choice. She was a deportee,' he said aloud, and again he felt a jab of a hot skewer in his chest.

However, one or two terrestrial cares remained, and the old man forced himself to think about the Tokarevs. From time to time his daugher and son-in-law had appeared at his bedside, but he had pretended not to notice them. And then he realized that while he was capable, that is, so long as he could still sign his name, he should make amends with Masha, on paper at least. He could be of some use yet: he could leave them the flat.

'A family exchange would be better,' said Tokarev, lowering his eyes. The delicate discussion was threatening to drag on, and Tokarev had only dropped in briefly with some curd cheese and a thermos for Pashet.

'What's a *family* exchange?' the old man demanded. As far as he was concerned, all that should have been necessary was his consent, and as for the ways and means thereafter – that was for the living to worry about.

His son-in-law, declining to sit down, started to explain that a family exchange was in essence a fictitious exchange of flats. Pashet would register officially at Masha's place, and Svetlana would move on paper to Pashet's address. But everyone would carry on living where they were, for the time being.

'*For the time being*? All right, goodbye. For the time being . . .' Pavel muttered, and lowered his feet on to the floor, although he was forbidden to get up.

'Why did you go and bring that up, mister?' asked a thin, unshaven lad who was lying diagonally opposite Cholyshev. With his hands behind his head, he was breathing heavily, as though he had just finished a game of football. He was actually a forward in a provincial team, and had suffered his first heart attack two years before, during a match. Since then the poor fellow had never left hospitals, had had a second heart attack, and now, in anticipation of a third, had managed to get into a Moscow hospital.

'Not your son, is he?' he said. 'Doesn't look like you, and treats you without respect.'

'He's my son-in-law,' replied Cholyshev, feeling guilty towards the footballer. Hospitals did not like taking in old people, but Zhenya had worked at this one, and Masha had immediately demanded – and obtained – a bed for her father by the window, where they had been intending to put the footballer.

'I couldn't figure it out at first,' said the forward. 'I knew there was something about him . . . Is he a Jew? Eh?'

'A baptized one,' said Cholyshev, without knowing why.

'That, dear colleague, doesn't change a thing. You know what they say about cured horses and forgiven thieves . . .' said a ringing voice on Pashet's left, where a thick-set little man with a shock of black and grey hair, and coal-black gypsy eyes was lying. 'Lying', however, was not quite the word to describe his position. Rather, he fidgeted, and did not even fidget for long at a time: he kept jumping up, running out to the corridor, coming back and dancing about between the beds, slapping his heels and thighs, singing ribald songs, and delighting in it all like a little boy hearing dirty words for the first time. 'You must have a bloody great nail up your arse, Filipp Semyonovich,' said the other patients in amazement.

'Did he change over long ago?' asked the gypsy-like man. 'My wife goes to church, too. But she's done that since she was a child . . .'

'Lots of people have turned to the church nowadays. It's fashionable . . .' said Cholyshev, knowing perfectly well that it was all much more serious and complicated than that. He was impatient to be left alone by his neighbour.

'Yes, fashion's a terrible thing,' agreed the lively Filipp Semyonovich. 'But a fashion, dear colleague, lasts only for a season or two – whereas people are allegedly predicting a religious revival. I'm afraid the new prophets will also be wide of the mark. You can't turn the clock back now. It's a pity, though: religion makes things easier. It's awful – you look around and all you see is thieving and drunkenness, drunkenness and thieving. There's no restraint. I would believe in God myself if He would restrain us by just one per cent – or two per cent in the case of those who are closer to the pie. Otherwise we'll plunder the whole country. In fact, it's beyond me how we haven't ruined Russia already! It's so long since we produced anything – all we do is consume and consume. We could do with the Church to prick our consciences. On the other hand, what could the Church do? It ruled Russia for a thousand years, and was overthrown in not much more than a day. Why? Can you explain it?'

'It didn't take root deeply enough . . .'

Worn out by sorrow and sleeplessness, the old man was not prepared for a discussion.

'Wasn't ten centuries enough?' grinned Filipp Semyonovich. 'No, it was because people's faith wasn't firm enough. They never revered God in Russia. What did Pushkin write? In "Gabrieliad" he has Christ as the son of the Devil.'

'That was just mischievousness. The madness of youth.'

'Ha! Some mischievousness . . . I'd like to see anybody today try to write that, say, we are the spiritual children not of Lenin, but of . . . Ah, it doesn't matter. No, Nicholas I* was a liberal: he forgave things like that. But what I don't get is this: if a hundred and fifty years ago clever people didn't believe in God, why should their descendants? I don't think they will. And if a few of them decide to get christened, quite honestly, it's because they haven't anything better to do, or else, like your son-in-law, they want to get rid of their Jewishness.'

'In the Kingdom of God there are neither Greeks nor Jews . . .'

'Yes, but we are not in the Kingdom of God, colleague, but in the Russian State, where life is impossible even for the Slavs, never mind the Jews.'

'But it's not easy for my son-in-law, believe me . . .'

'Of course it is, colleague. I'm a Jew myself.' (The lively fellow softened his voice to a whisper.) 'I didn't get baptized, it's true. I was in the Komsomol – "Down, down with rabbis, down, down with popes!" Did you sing it too? Religion inside out. When were you born? 1902? I'm ten years younger. In my wisdom I almost joined the Party. But luckily they packed me off to prison. No, not for long. I was in exile for longer. I trained as a mechanic, came to my senses, and then the war started and my convictions were waived . . . Were you at the front? A colonel? Ah, a captain? That's not much. Where? That was convenient. Didn't you . . .' (Here he lowered his voice even further.) '. . . think of buggering off? No, not from Harbin, from Vienna . . .'

'It never occurred to me,' said Cholyshev with a black look – not merely because the conversation was becoming rather risky, but because it was closing in on the time of Nadya's departure, and therefore on Zhenya's death.

'When I was in Germany I couldn't sleep for thinking about it, but I never did. I felt sorry for my wife. We'd only met just before

† Reactionary Russian tsar from 1825 to 1855, under whose strict censorship many writers, including Pushkin, suffered. [Tr.]

the war. When I got back I realized she wasn't worth returning for. I married again, and she was no better. It was only after the third that it sank in that women are a rotten bunch. Now I keep them at a distance. No attachments. Sleep with them once and that's your lot. In general, I only go in for the youngsters now. They're easier-going. What about you?'

'I've swum my lot.'

'You've what?'

'Somewhere in Tolstoy, some children shout to an old man to come and swim with them in a pond, and he says: "I've swum my lot." '

'That's tough. If I get out of here I'm going to try my own treatment. You know how they treat old men in the East? They put a young girl on either side of him.'

'There aren't enough to go round. Look at how many pensioners there are . . .'

'But what's the sexual revolution for, if not for that?!' the 'gypsy' laughed, but suddenly turned gloomy. 'I had two "warnings". Even the medicos missed them. They said, "Sorry, Filipp Semyonovich, but you had your heart attacks standing up . . ." Have you had any "warnings"? No? Have I alarmed you? Have a rest. You can do that here . . .'

I could do that at home, thought Cholyshev; but this is home now . . . He turned on to his right side and covered his head: the sun was annoying him. This would be the way to go. A quiet death under a hospital blanket and a grey washed-out sheet. Unobtrusively, causing no bother to anyone, straight to the mortuary, and then to the new crematorium outside Moscow. No funeral service like Bronka's. Zhenya won't be there, to 'bend her curly head and cry', like Donna Anna . . . Zhenya had straight hair . . . I killed her. I, alone. It was from me that she ran away across the ocean, and at her age one shouldn't run . . .

The following day Pashet told his daughter about the family exchange. The restless Filipp Semyonovich, in the next bed, turned round demonstratively, but Cholyshev felt that he was picking up every word.

'What nonsense,' said Masha angrily. 'Svetlana is only sixteen. Who's going to give her a separate flat? Lie at peace and stop thinking up wild schemes.'

'But something has to be done . . .'

'Yes, but not just any old thing. I hate half-measures.'

'Then do as you think best . . .'

The old man had sat up in bed to make his voice sound firmer, and he noticed Filipp Semyonovich's back twitching with displeasure.

'. . . Greyness, tedium, cold. My God, what ties me to all this?' wrote Tokarev in a dog-eared ledger. He was sitting in his small, eight-square-metres room, in a five-storey concrete-panel block of flats. Outside it was indeed grey, tedious and cold. An invisible drizzle was pouring on to piles of empty boxes which had been thrown into a ravine, and nothing seemed to exist on Earth except the ravine and the boxes.

'I hate this time of year when it is neither winter nor autumn. If only it would pour with snow,' Grisha continued to write. 'Seven weeks ago, when we moved in here, I stood in front of this window and, despite the haste, and Zhenya's death, and Pashet's illness, I could feel God. Out there beyond the boxes, the sky was blue and descended towards me. There was something eternal and at the same time youthful in it, as thought it had just been created, but for the rest of time. I did not wish to become immersed in my diary then, but rather to suck in my sky through the wide-open window and wait for the time when I would step across the windowsill and walk over this blue field just as simply as I walk on the ground. No, not my soul, but I myself, exactly as I am here in this room . . .

'But now the rain, or drizzle (through two unwashed panes one cannot tell which!) fogs the space and fills me with loathing for this place. And I no longer can see God . . .

'But how good it was with him! Everything was close at hand,

and I was inseparable from the Russian people and forgave them all injuries, old and new . . . But then, so stupidly, Zheka died, Masha was sacked, the weather changed, old fears came back to me, and I again was aware of how alien I am here. That was how it was after the Literary Institute, when I was not given work. But at that time I thought it was because of my biography, and not my nationality. Only during Khrushchev's thaw did I realize: it is better to spend time in camp than be born in Jew. Jewishness means alienation for the whole of your life – and your children's lives, and perhaps your grandchildren's lives.

'One evening Pashet, my daughter and I were hurrying through the empty streets of a small town to catch the last train when suddenly we heard drunken voices behind our backs. Svetka pressed herself against me, but I could not calm her – I was afraid myself. Pashet, on the other hand, marched on as though nothing were amiss, and argued with me without lowering his voice. I conjectured that he was calm not because he was old and not afraid of death; he was simply sure that his own people – Russians – would not touch him. And they did indeed walk past.

'In the train I praised Pashet. Drunks were like dogs, I said: they could smell when someone was afraid of them. I confessed to him that when I hear swearing at night I always expect to be beaten up . . .

'Pashet frowned. My frankness evidently offended him. As a matter of fact, to this day he cannot fathom why I got baptized. He says I have been trying to squeeze the "Yid" out of me all my life. But is it my fault that I do not feel any blood tie with the Jews? I do not want to think badly of my relations, but what if Alf was too stingy with the doctors and that's why they did not save Zheka . . . And how was she buried? What kind of headstone have they given her? Or was she cremated? In which case, where is the urn? Nadka doesn't write, and I am ashamed to look my father-in-law in the eyes, as though it was I who had sent Zheka to America.

'. . . Oh well, let Pashet think what he likes about my baptism. But I am a member of the Russian intelligentsia, and parochialism, and Jewish pragmatism and conceit are, to be honest, foreign to me. I was nurtured on the literature of Russia, and my God is the God of the Russian people!

'. . . Masha and I turned to the Orthodox Church, and paid for it at once. Someone informed the institute about Varvara Alekseyevna's funeral. They were running a competition: Masha, naturally, was failed, and now she cannot find a job anywhere. My work continues not to be published, and we have no money. On top of that, we have moved to this terrible flat with its foreign dirt and smells. I can imagine how "up-tight" Pashet must be. He is to be discharged in a day or two. It is simply indecent to keep an old man in hospital any longer . . .

'The previous occupiers of the flat volunteered to do it up themselves. But Masha was in a hurry, fearing that Pashet might pass away at any moment. She took money instead of the repairs and then blew the money . . . We shouldn't have exchanged flats. How will Pashet get up to the fourth floor? He should never have been put in hospital in the first place: he could have rested in bed at home, since they found nothing critical in his health.

'As it is I have taken the separate room promised to Pashet and moved a desk up to the window, and now I shall be sorry to move into the communicating room.* People are rascals – they get used to their comforts . . .

'It is after six o'clock: time to take Pashet his food. Although what we cook here is probably no more nutritious than hospital food . . .'

Tokarev did not get up immediately upon closing the ledger. He had no desire to go to the hospital. The fourth Arab–Israeli war had just died down, and the antipathy towards Jews whipped up by the newspapers and television was keenly felt in the ward.

* 'Communicating rooms', i.e. rooms giving access to other rooms, are fairly common in Soviet flats, and are generally disliked because in most cases they serve as bedrooms for some members of the family, as well as sitting-rooms during the day. [Tr.]

Moreover, the patients there had recently been joined by a puny young Jew with a hooked nose and curly sidelocks, who had applied to emigrate. Tokarev felt constrained in his presence.

Luckily, the young Jew had gone out somewhere, but the footballer was letting off steam. 'These skunks are lucky: they shit here and then escape to their own country . . .'

Tokarev's appearance did not disconcert him.

'Stop that!' said Cholyshev to the footballer. 'And you go away,' he whispered to his son-in-law, but Grisha continued to unpack the food he had brought.

'I won't say anything out of turn, mister. Some of them aren't so bad. But this one sold his motherland.'

'Hey! Who's this giving a concert?' came a roar from the door. And, letting through a tall young woman, Filipp Semyonovich came into the room with his arm round another Jew wearing glasses. 'Who sold his motherland?' he demanded, holding his elbows against his sides, as though spoiling for a fight.

The footballer sullenly hunched his back.

'Just watch it! If I hear that again I'll carve you up,' threatened the gypsy-like Filipp.

'Have you gone off your head?' asked a man who was lying by the other window. He was not really in for the treatment he was receiving, but rather trying his best to fall seriously ill. He would stick his head out of the window for long periods and gulp in the damp November air. An inspection was being carried out at his factory.

'What are you grumbling about, Filipp?' the malingerer repeated. 'What the lad said was right. You get different types of Jew. Two of them rent my dacha every summer: they're decent enough.'

'I suppose you rip them off?'

'No! They're just like us . . . But those who emigrate are traitors.'

'You are speaking nonsense,' declared an authoritative voice, evidently more accustomed to shouting, in the opposite corner. A corpulent man had been lying there since morning: apparently a fairly high-ranking chief, because asked whether he would prefer the window wide open or just a little, he replied that he couldn't care less as a separate ward was being freed for him in the evening.

'To hell with them if they leave! Or would you prefer them to stay?' smirked the corpulent comrade.

'Mark, pay no attention,' said the young woman loudly. She had not yet sat down, and Tokarev admired her fine figure and legs, neatly tucked into tall suede boots.

What a pity, he thought; Pashet is being discharged, and I shan't meet her again. What a beautiful face! And she doesn't look at all Jewish . . .

The woman turned to the malingerer: 'Did I hear you baiting Mark?'

'Lena, calm down,' said the young Jew.

'Don't you worry, miss . . . Hey, do you hear?' Filipp Semyonovich addressed the whole ward. 'Let me repeat: the first person who insults Mark will get a couple of almighty uppercuts and I'll personally supervise the exit of his corpse from this ward!' Filipp rolled his pyjama sleeve up to his bicep.

'Shut up, Filipp. This is a hospital, not a boxing ring,' said the footballer hoarsely. 'Nobody's touching you, so keep out of it.'

'Why should I keep out of it, when I'm a Jew myself?'

'Come off it! Why didn't you say before? No-o, you're having us on . . .?' The forward's voice lacked conviction.

'What's that if it's not Jewish!' exclaimed the lively gypsy with enthusiasm, and Tokarev sensed how proud Filipp was not to be concealing his nationality any more. I could be like that . . . he thought bitterly; but what can I do? Threaten to beat them up? But this is a hospital, after all. And discusssions are pointless. They consider me foreign, though I was born here and have possibly suffered more than any of them. It's all right for Pashet: he is one of them. And it's all right for Lena: she's headed for Palestine with her Zionist. But what about me? But what a striking woman she is . . . Passionate; her eyes burn . . . No wonder

Filipp was showing off in front of her.

Something had indeed snapped inside Filipp: 'Ah, my children, I look at you and grow younger. There you are: my people! You are leaving, and will give birth to a real Israeli Jew, a Sabra.'

'He'll drop dead out there. It's too hot!' sneered the footballer.

'He hasn't died here: he'll last a hundred years out there. Our climate is worse.'

'Oh, give us a break, Filipp!'

The footballer got down from his bed and sauntered towards the door.

'Mind you don't peg out yourself!' laughed Filipp Semyonovich. 'Ah, Mark, when I look at you I remember my childhood. There were fellows like you in our village: they were called *Yeshibotniki*, or Jewish seminarists. They were treated like saints: it was considered a great honour to give shelter and food to a *Yeshibotnik*. They used to move from one house to another, like nomads. And you look just like them, Mark, with your glasses and sidelocks.'

'He's a Candidate of Science!'* laughed the young woman. She was squatting in front of her husband's bedside cabinet, tidying it up. Tokarev could not tear his eyes away from her. He was surprised at himself: What's it all about?! I'm at a total loss. Admittedly, I have finished my 'Attempt at Biography', but I haven't the faintest idea what to do with it. Now I have started work on a long novel, and I'm terrified that the flat might be searched. The KGB probably have their eyes on me. We have no money and none forthcoming. I suppose I could send the 'Biography' abroad, but would they accept it? Here they don't publish me because I'm not one of 'them'; and who needs me in the West? But supposing the 'Biography' was published – and made no impact? What then? I'd have no money, no fame – only a certain notoriety among a few KGB officers . . . And time is running out. Both here and abroad they publish all sorts of rubbish, and yet Grigory Tokarev might as well not exist; my name is already forgotten. And suddenly after all these catastrophes I

* Equivalent of Doctor of Philosophy. [Tr.]

can't take my eyes off another woman! Is it ridiculous? Or miraculous, perhaps? Maybe my salvation lies in her!?

'What's this?!' shrieked Lena, and pulled from under a pile of books a sheet of paper on which Tokarev could just make out a clumsily drawn skull and crossbones.

' "Fuck off to Israel, Yid-features, or else we'll cut off the rest, too!" ' she read aloud. 'Did you write this?!' she pounced on the malingerer.

'I don't go in for anonymous letters,' he replied with dignity.

'Someone from the next ward put it there,' sighed Filipp Semyonovich.

Mark shrugged it off with a smile: 'It's only what you'd expect, after all.'

'Nonsense,' said Filipp.

'No, it's not nonsense, it's reality. Anti-Semitism never disappeared, you know: it was merely laid aside for a short time. But after the war, Filipp Semyonovich, it showed its true colours. At first they blocked our access to the universities and privileged higher educational establishments, then to the less privileged ones. Then they stopped employing us. Now they harass us with red tape. Soon they'll be shouting "Beat the Jews!" and start saving Russia by methods their forebears resorted to . . .'

'Mark, you mustn't get excited,' said the woman.

'I'm perfectly calm, Lena. I'm merely explaining to Filipp Semyonovich why we have decided to leave . . . Don't think we're leaving out of fear; in Israel there are no fewer dangers. It's just that we suddenly realized that here we are superfluous . . . Three generations of Jewish intellectuals dreamt of becoming part of Russian life. They renounced their God and their notions of being a "chosen people". They had only one passion – to become Russian. It seemed they succeeded in this. They raved about Tolstoy, and even Dostoyevsky – yes, Dostoyevsky despite his anti-Semitism. They – and we, too, the fourth generation – regarded Russia as their motherland and themselves as Russians. We attributed the hostility of certain sections of the populace and the leadership either to the backwardness of the former or to the latter's forced reaction to the schemes of so-called international Zionism. But what shocked me, Lena and all of our friends most of all was the hatred shown us not by some riff-raff or bureaucrats, but by real intellectuals. Yes – by writers, poets, artists, and physicists like myself, who dismissed us unreservedly as alien, rootless, or even harmful for Russia . . . And then we understood: there was nothing to hope for, and went back to our forgotten roots. We remembered that we were the chosen people with our own destiny, we started cramming Hebrew and studying the Talmud, and painfully and grudgingly casting off Russia, we applied to emigrate.'

'Why are they so nervous?' grumbled the corpulent man. 'Imagine: just because they're squeezed a little, they get into a flap about "us" and "them"! What would they have been like if they'd had to suffer a famine like we did in '33?'

'If they would at least let us out at once . . .' said the young woman. 'But you never know until the last minute whether they will agree . . . And as for famine,' she turned to the corpulent man, 'you can't scare me with that. I kept up a hunger strike for eight days.'

'You poor girl,' said Filipp Semyonovich sympathetically.

'Idiots,' said the fat man. 'They should let them all out. All of them. We'd get rid of them at last . . .'

'Exactly,' agreed the malingerer.

'I sympathize with you, Mark,' Cholyshev entered the discussion. He felt constrained by his son-in-law's presence, but in view of the corpulent man's shameless talk he also found it awkward to remain silent. 'It's bad that in Russia everyone is divided into "natives" and "strangers". But I'm afraid that in Israel too you might end up as strangers. Every nation has its share of prejudices.'

'The Jews aren't a nation,' grinned the malingerer.

'My God, you head's full of Stalinist junk,' laughed the lively Filipp Semyonovich. 'Let us listen to sensible people. What were you going to say about Israel, Pashka?'

'That it has complications of its own. I have a fair idea of what its citizens are like – or at least the ones who left here straight after the Civil War. It wasn't easy to get out then, either. Only the most desperate took the plunge. Do you remember?' he asked Filipp Semyonovich without returning the use of his first name.

'No. I ran away from home. My mates were keener on joining the Komsomol or the Party.'

'The Trotskyites and Zinovievites, you mean . . .' said the malingerer jeeringly.

'Exactly,' retorted a voice from the other corner.

'It's easy enough to say "exactly", but without the Trotskys I doubt if you would have landed a separate ward,' said Filipp Semyonovich, casting a malevolent glance in that direction.

'But my grandfather was a cattle-dealer. I'd have survived anyway,' said the corpulent man with a wry smile.

'So you see, Mark,' Cholyshev continued, 'it was the most determined and courageous people who left for Palestine, but they were – if you'll forgive me – provincial townspeople, from the *shtetls*, not intellectuals. It was easier for them to get up and go. Their roots weren't particularly deep here and, frankly, they had nothing to thank Russia for. They led secluded lives, barely communicating with the outside world, which they neither cared about much nor understood. I fear they may not have changed since they settled in Palestine, and still divide people with the same *shtetl* mentality into "us" and "them", "natives" and "strangers". They're undoubtedly brave, and tremendous fighters, but you see they can't achieve peace with the Arabs. It evidently all stems from that same provincial narrow-mindedness and conceit, from their unwillingness to understand the enemy and their problems.'

'That's slanderous! Israel is led by educated people with European values!' Mark even flushed with indignation.

'Stop this! He mustn't get excited,' said the young woman angrily.

'OK. Shhh! No argument!' said Filipp Semyonovich, jokingly throwing up his hands. 'Well done, kids. I'm envious of you for going. But I – sinner that I am – fell in love with Russia and its women. What can I do! My first wife was Russian, so was my second, so was my third. My daughters are registered as Russians, and my grandchildren probably don't even guess that their granddad is a Semite. The Jewish soul seems to have a soft spot for the Slavs, eh?' He winked at the malingerer. 'Of course, it happens the other way around, too. What do you say? I don't know about your younger daughter, but your elder one has a touch of Jewishness about her, hasn't she?'

'Well? The eldest is supposed to be the best,' sniggered the malingerer.

'There's nothing funny about it,' boomed the chief. 'Producing half-breeds . . . neither fish nor fowl. As far as I'm concerned, that type is the worst of the lot.'

Poor Svetlana, Tokarev thought about his daughter. That animal doesn't even look at my cross. What difference does a cross make to him, when his hatred is zoological?'

'We should turf them out, every one of them,' concluded the corpulent grandson of a cattle-dealer.

'So you don't intend to burn them?' asked Filipp.

'I fought against Hitler,' frowned the fat chief. 'But I don't abuse everything German indiscriminately. Even he had his uses.'

'Getting rid of his Jews, for instance?' Filipp Semyonovich turned pale.

'What do I care about Jews over there when I see too many of them here?'

'. . . Nevertheless, Pavel Rodionovich, Israel is a typical Western state,' Mark repeated.

'The Israelis ought to be less arrogant,' sighed Filipp. 'Pashka is right. They have to try and achieve peace with the Arabs.'

'And with the Palestinians?' Mark flared up.

'Especially with them. They could establish some sort of limit or buffer zone.'

'Arafat will never agree to it . . .'

'Then find someone else who's more compliant.'

'E-hey . . .' said the voice in the corner. 'You curse Hitler, but look for quislings.'

'And you're for the Arabs, are you?' asked Filipp.

'No. I don't give a damn about them. It would suit me if all the black, yellow and other children of various races got the hell out of here. Those who have washed their hands of us should be allowed to push off; those who haven't should be forced.'

'Exactly,' said the malingerer joyfully.

'And what will you do with your half-Jewish daughter?' asked Filipp, smiling wryly.

'Let them all take comfort, Filipp Semyonovich, from the fact that as soon as Mark is better we shall be setting out for that supposedly narrow-minded state,' said Lena, and she embraced her husband.

'You've got me all wrong,' said Cholyshev in embarrassment. 'I have every sympathy for your future homeland. Reuniting a people after twenty centuries is a great feat. But what worries me is this: during those twenty centuries the world has been almost exclusively Christian. And the Jews, by striving to retain their religion and their distinctiveness, have naturally passed by –'

'Christianity is one of the offshoots of Judaism!' Mark interrupted the old man.

'Hardly! But even if that's so, then the offshoot has become the main branch, and by rejecting Christianity you lose two thousand years of spiritual experience. I am not as orthodox as my son-in-law,' the old man nodded at Tokarev, 'but all my bearings, all my standards of good and evil, and probably yours too, are Christian. And in Israel, which really is a miracle-state, erected on the blood of pogroms, the ashes of Auschwitz, and the hatred of all anti-Semites, I'm afraid you may miss the Saviour.'

'But we don't intend to forget Him,' said the young woman.

'No, no,' grinned Filipp. 'Forget all that . . . Without Judaism how will you make them stick together, all these people from Germany, Africa, Bokhara, Georgia – and Russia? You're surrounded by a hundred million Arabs plus the little problem of oil.

So confront the green banner of Islam with your own white one with its six-pointed star! And there's no place for Christ in Judaea after two thousand years, even if He was born there.'

'You're absolutely wrong. Israel is a democratic country,' objected Mark, becoming more agitated. 'Everything is possible in a democracy. Even Judo-Christianity. I know such people.'

'Just look at that: they've got everything!' said the malingerer in wonderment.

The corpulent man apparently wanted to add his own comment, but he suddenly went pale, sat up in bed, and snatched his woollen chequered dressing-gown from the rail.

'What are you doing? You're forbidden to move!' exclaimed the malingerer, but the chief merely waved his hand and dashed out of the ward.

'That's enough arguing . . . Look what we've reduced the fellow to . . .' said the malingerer with a yawn.

'You should have brought him a bed-pan if you're so sorry for him,' said Filipp.

'He wouldn't use it in front of the girl . . .'

'Call him back. I'll go out,' Lena offered.

The trifles of hospital life . . . thought Tokarev. How on earth did Pashet get on in here? Neither Masha nor I greased the nurses' palms. The poor man is so unassertive, he probably suffered . . . Tokarev glanced timidly at his father-in-law, who was lying perfectly aloof.

All of a sudden the door burst open and the footballer dragged in the cattle-dealer's grandson, looking thinner and smaller in his flapping dressing-gown.

'Hh, Hh, Hh . . .' he was panting, almost groaning.

Tokarev started counting for some reason. 'One, two, three . . .' The second-hand of his watch completed a quarter of the circle as the chief wheezed for the ninth time. Almost like a pulse, thought Tokarev.

'Don't worry! Be a man, that's the main thing!' Filipp Semyonovich went up to the chief's bed, but the latter did not seem to hear him, and continued half-groaning, half-sobbing.

Six . . . eight . . . twelve . . . Tokarev went on counting. Forty-eight puffs a minute. Now they sounded like gurgles, as though water was bubbling into his lungs.

'He's going to be sick. Get him a bed-pan,' said Filipp, but the malingerer turned to face the window, and the footballer lay out flat on his bed. He seemed to have been affected too.

'Turn round, my girl. I'll deal with this hero.' Filipp winked to Mark's wife and drew out a porcelain vessel from under the bed. 'Come on, lad. Two fingers in the mouth and away we go . . . Er, you've turned green already . . . Somebody fetch the doctor quickly!'

Mark's wife ran out into the corridor and came back with an impatient woman doctor. Having chased Filipp away, the doctor sat down on the corpulent patient's bed and set about taking his blood pressure.

'But he'll choke!' said Filipp Semyonovich.

'Don't try to teach me. You're getting in the way . . .' The woman doctor blushed. The blood-pressure gauge was causing her some difficulty as the rubber tube kept falling out of the bulb.

'Call the sister. Tell her to bring his case history!' she shouted. She sounded perplexed.

The night sister, a spirited lass with a considerable and almost uncovered bust, had already clearly had one too many to drink, but she tried not to let on and bustled around efficiently. She immediately brought a large syringe and planted it in the corpulent man's buttock.

'Is that any easier, dear?' she asked in a surprisingly tender way.

'No-o, be-ed-pa-an . . .' the cattle-dealer's descendant filtered through the sobs.

'Sit down, love, sit down . . .' The nurse raised him by his shoulders.

'Put a screen round,' said the doctor. She was obstinately leafing through the case notes, but glancing up at the brisk sister she added self-importantly: 'Injections won't help. Bring a drip.'

'Call someone else,' said the young nurse gaily, and a second nurse wheeled in a yellow screen.

Just like the one that was round Varvara Alekseyevna, Tokarev recalled. It's a pity I didn't take a look at her. I missed her death, and a writer has no right to neglect such experience. Is this fellow really going to die too?

Tokarev could see nothing from his father-in-law's bedside. The cattle-dealer's grandson was totally hidden by the screen, apart from his elbow, which stuck out, white and pitted with psoriasis, like pumice-stone. Tokarev no longer felt any malice towards the man. It had given way to curiosity. He had even ceased looking at Lena, who was sitting with her back to him, shielding from Mark the crowd of nurses in the ward and the burly resuscitation specialist. He had the physique of a weight-lifter, rosy cheeks and a moustache, and Tokarev looked at him in admiration, thinking: I bet he could even bring you back from the gates of Hell! The resuscitator seemed to be in a jolly mood, as though he were preparing for something pleasant – barbecueing kebabs, say – rather than for a struggle with a half-dead body.

'Of course, there's no oxygen,' said the burly resuscitator, turning a tap on the wall. 'Bring in our stuff,' he nodded to a young nurse, evidently his assistant.

Both leaves of the ward door burst open and the drip was wheeled in, followed by a trolley of syringes and bottles, and another trolley with instruments which Tokarev did not recognize. Then the young nurse went behind the screen with something made of black leather which looked like a cross between a bag and a saddle.

'Come on, push, don't be lazy,' the weight-lifter encouraged his assistant, and through a crack in the screen Tokarev saw the girl hunched over the strange black object, squeezing it as though she were washing clothes.

'Keep going!' the resuscitator went on, but his voice was no longer cheerful. 'Cut his shirt open,' he said more softly. 'On the right . . . Further right.'

'Don't look,' old Cholyshev whispered to his son-in-law, but Grisha was craning his neck quite indecorously.

'They've stuck it straight into his chest!' said the malingerer to Tokarev with a conspiratorial wink. He could see everything. 'They just snipped the skin with scissors, and away it went!'

Tokarev had himself noticed that the liquid in the drip had started bubbling like boiling water.

'Once they pump in the solution he'll be as good as new . . .' said the malingerer with delight.

'That's enough chattering!' said the resuscitator angrily. 'Turn round, man. It's not a TV show.' He stuck his head out from behind the screen and wagged his finger at the malingerer, then gave a tired sigh. 'There's no room here, and it's upsetting the patients. Take him to intensive care, girls.'

Once again there was a stir of activity. One trolley was pushed to the window, the other out into the corridor, the screen was folded up, and the bed containing the unfortunate white-faced cattle-dealer's grandson, who could certainly no longer be called corpulent, floated slowly and solemnly, like a catafalque, out of the ward.

'No more quarrelling,' wheezed the footballer.

'Mm-hm,' said Filipp, and both threw unfriendly glances at Tokarev, although he had not opened his mouth all evening.

Their arguments are over, thought Grisha. Before death they are all united and I am again an outsider to them because I am not ill. Whatever happens, I'm an outsider . . .

With a listless nod of the head to Pashet, Tokarev went down to the vestibule, put on his coat, and decided to wait for Mark's wife. The cloakroom attendant, making allowances for his ragged coat, did not drive him out into the cold.

Finally he heard the click of boots on the staircase, and snatching the young woman's fur coat from the attendant he helped her to put it on.

'Thank you,' said Lena. Her shoulders twitched, and Grisha realized she was slightly drunk.

The woman was buttoning her coat, and he could not let her go away alone. The usual phrases for such situations – 'Where do you come from?' 'Where have you been all my life?' – were no good. He needed something sincere, serious and penetrating. Then in a whisper, so that the cloakroom lady would not hear, but without concealing his excitement, Tokarev asked: 'So you are leaving?'

'Yes, we've washed our hands of the place, as that bastard put it – I'm sorry, that poor chap, I mean,' Lena grinned ironically, and Grisha took heart. After all, he had not been sure whether this woman would speak to him. In the ward he had behaved indifferently, and after his father-in-law's comment Lena might have concluded that since he was baptized he could be classed with the anti-Semites.

'We've washed our hands,' she repeated, 'but Mark had a small heart attack.'

As a result of the stress caused by the Visa Office: how could a weakling like that take on the Russian State? thought Tokarev. He led the woman out into the hospital yard, which was lightened by the slowly flying snow and round, dull lamps. What weather! – he rejoiced. You couldn't wish for better! The start of winter is the start of love! That's it – not another word about Mark!

But in the spacious black and white yard, Lena, in her light dog-hair coat and socklike knitted hat, seemed even more inaccessible to the poor, ragged Grisha than she had done in the ward. Once again he felt his eternal helplessness: God, how can I attract such a woman? I scarcely exist. Masha exists, with her drunken outbursts and tears. Svetlana exists, with her whims, her bad marks, and her wayward character. They have either absorbed me, or grown through me. I am a poor imitation of the old Tokarev. How can I, as I am now, attract such a woman?

None the less he seized what chance there was: 'But aren't you sorry to leave all *this*?' He drew his hand around the lifeless prisms of the white concrete hospital blocks, which looked dark against the snow.

'I used to wonder about that, but now I'm sure I shan't be sorry . . .'

'But what if you do start missing it?'

'It's out of the question. But you wouldn't understand that . You are a poor Jew . . . Don't be offended. If it wasn't for Mark, I would have become a poor Jew, too. I'd probably have got christened like you.'

I've hooked her, though, thought Tokarev more cheerfully, not even annoyed that the woman saw baptism as something unworthy.

'I lived very badly, always bustling about. I lost myself, and got nothing in return. Have you found yourself in the Orthodox Church?'

'I'm looking . . .' Tokarev was put out of countenance.

'I'm sorry: I'm not just asking out of curiosity. I really would like to know. What prompted you to take that step? I mean, you're clever. Mark told me that you are a critic and that your name is Tokarev. I remember your articles well – the whole of our class used to read them. Why do I never come across your name these days? Have you been banned because you got baptized? Or, on the contrary, did you get baptized in protest at not being published? Or did you actually start believing in God? But then, God and the Church are not the same thing . . .'

'Yes they are . . .' Tokarev almost objected, but realized that an argument would sidetrack them. One day he would explain it all to her. He would tell her how back in his distant childhood he had had doubts about the justice of the City Party Committee: the villa, the electric toys and the blue bicycle; about how he saw his father's misfortune as a kind of retribution; about how he had admired the Russian people in Siberia – their openness, their carefree attitude to the future, and their almost childlike certainty that everything would work out well for them and their country (and in the middle of such a war!); he would tell this wonderful Lena how his new love for Russia extinguished his former dream, inherited from his mother, of world revolution. (Later, when they declared the restoration of 'Leninist norms', he was glad that his father's sullied name was cleared, but the 'norms' themselves meant nothing to him because he had lost faith in Marxism.) One day he would confess to Lena how he had suddenly grown lonely, cold and scared, as though finding himself in a strange courtyard in the middle of the night . . . This was his country. He had never seen any other, and knew no other language. Even his knowledge of foreign history was pretty sketchy. He belonged here. This was his Russia, and the faith of Russia, the faith of Dostoyevsky, was his faith – whatever Dostoyevsky had written about Jews. (And anyway, Dostoyevsky had in mind a different type of consciousness!) Lena would understand everything . . .

But now, stopping and turning the woman to face him, he hoarsely breathed out the simplest explanation: 'Why did I start believing? From fear . . . From fear, that's all . . .'

He wished he could embrace the woman, to drown all his sorrow and despair in her, but he felt it was still too early: it might miscarry . . . And although Lena was quite close he merely whispered, ardently and hurriedly: 'From fear . . . It is terrible without God . . . I realized this once in an aeroplane . . . We ran into some turbulence. All around there was lightning and thick cloud. It all comes flying at you. The plane bumps up and down and lurches from side to side, and you are helpless, unprotected, and humiliated . . .'

Getting carried away with himself, Tokarev forgot that he did not fly often, and had never hit turbulence, and was relating not his own experiences, but Pashet's. It had happened the autumn before last, when Pashet and Zhenya were returning from the Crimea, and their plane could not land for a long time. Pashet had likened the bumpy flight to life on earth, and Tokarev now enthusiastically expounded the old man's reflections to Lena: 'Do you understand how unhappy one is in a jolting airliner? The floor under your feet isn't a floor, but a semblance of a floor. Outside the thin covering is – brrr . . . – cold death. But the passengers sit flicking through magazines, or else gaze with curiosity through the windows. The thunder, the lightning, the clouds racing furiously past – the whole of this apocalypse outside the windows does not worry them in the least. They believe in the dependability of the plane and the experience of its captain . . . And it's the same in our life: there is so much thunder, speed, horror and despair around, but if you believe in the rationality of the universe and the goodness of God, you have no fear, however much you are shaken or thrown about. Am I speaking clearly?'

'Eloquently, I should say,' the young woman smiled sadly. 'Too eloquently. But I understand you. You are being very frank with me somehow, as though you are intentionally throwing yourself open. That's probably because you are also unhappy . . .'

The room had about thirteen square metres, but two of the walls were spoilt by ordinary doors, and the third by a door on to the balcony, so there was no room for Cholyshev's wide day-bed. They made up Svetlana's short divan-bed for the old man. The wall against which he lay was not next to the stair-well, but he could hear doors being banged on all five floors. Either the building had developed cracks or it had been put together badly in the first place – and Pashet had developed insomnia in his old age, and his hearing was as keen as ever.

There was, in fact, a good deal to hinder his sleep. The old man had not expected the flat to be so run-down. The wallpaper was greasy and stained, and – especially at the bottom – badly torn. The previous occupiers must have had a dog. The kitchen was so dirty it was unpleasant to eat there. The bath was rusty, and, imagining a dog being washed in it not so very long ago, the old man washed standing up, spraying water all over the floor.

'Don't bother wiping it up! I'll do it!' Masha shouted through the door. 'And don't dare go washing your underclothes. You'll just make a mess, or soak the neighbours down below. I'll wash them out later.'

It was a three-roomed flat. But the only separate room was taken by Grisha; Masha and her daughter shared the tiny bedroom off the main room, and old Cholyshev was stuck out on a limb, getting in everyone's way. At night he could not sleep, and he suffered during the day, until he finally remembered about the balcony. Now he would pull on every conceivable article of clothing, take a stool out to the balcony (there was no room for a chair) and sit there for hours like a watchman. Being shy of passers-by, he rarely looked down, and usually stared into the distance, at the ravine with its mountains of boxes, or up into the grey sky. To prevent draughts, they closed the balcony door behind him, but he sensed that one or other of the family was always peering through the glass to check that he had not died or jumped over the railing. He was quite prepared to die, but he had no desire to roll about on the pavement like a bedraggled doll wrapped up in scarves and shawls . . .

I'm like a wild animal in an open-air cage, thought Cholyshev. Four floors up without a lift – that's what my death looks like . . .

Perhaps he might have summoned up the courage to go down on to the street, and would have returned without hurrying, stopping on each half-landing to lean against the wall and rest. But then he would have been made to take out the rubbish, and go to the shops, or the laundry, or goodness knows what all. So he plumped for the cramped little balcony. This cradle, unreliably welded to the wall, became his last refuge. Sometimes, like a child, losing his sense of reality, the old man imagined that from here it was not so far through the air to America, and thus to Zhenya. But his ravings would end. Cholyshev would rap on the windowpane, and if it was his granddaughter who opened the door she would grumble about the draught: 'We should seal up the balcony door. Otherwise I'll never get rid of these colds, and I won't get my school certificate.'

'You won't get your school certificate because you're too busy with other things,' Cholyshev answered her in his mind. He already knew a thing or two about his granddaughter. One day, when her mother and father were out, Svetlana had locked herself up with the telephone in the separate room.

'So you passed? Good marks? Ah, you don't know yet . . .' Svetlana chattered, forgetting that the walls carried her voice perfectly. 'Do you ever stop working? Clever boy. You're a clever boy, I said. How am I? Not very well. Just because. No, not the school. My parents? Hm . . . I'm not like them. I'm a nun. Don't laugh . . . OK, not a nun; a hermit, then. I don't go out anywhere, like Granddad . . . He's fine – he got over it. No, it was the old crones who kicked the bucket . . . Macabre? What's that? Ah, when you laugh about death. Well, that's why I'm laughing – because I don't want to live. Are you interested? Why didn't you phone before if you're interested? Oh, you lost the new number? That was convenient! Why? Because I've got the same as I had in the spring . . . You don't remember? Well, you should do. I said you should remember. It does concern you too. Got it?! Well?'

So that's why Masha didn't ask her to Bronka's funeral! She was recovering from an abortion. Sixteen years – what a fatal year . . . The old man sighed, suddenly feeling guilty towards his grand-daughter. He had never dandled her or helped to raise her. Masha would not let Zhenya within a mile of Svetlana, and Cholyshev had held back out of solidarity. He had only given her presents: prams, clothes, and government bonds.

'Well, have you swallowed your tongue? Is it tasty? Don't worry . . . Oh, you're brave! And what do you advise? Your grandmother? No thanks! What am I phoning for? Not to hear your lectures. I don't care what you think. Neither do you? I don't believe you. It doesn't bother me, but it bothers you. You're a coward. *I* don't give a damn about anything. About you, or the school, or anybody at all!' she shouted behind the wall. 'I will prove it. I'll go away. No, not to the Crimea – what's so special about that? It's raining there. America – that's where I'll go! My aunt is coming for me.'

Surely they haven't invited Nadka? – Cholyshev took fright. So that was why Tokarev was hinting about 'what a good idea it would be, Pashet, to freshen up the flat, or at least change the wallpaper'. 'Freshen up'! It's like spraying a filthy, sweaty man who hasn't washed for years, with eau-de-Cologne. And with what money, if you please? Everything went on Zhenya's trip. Would Nadka really come? At least Alf might dissuade her again. A year

159

before he had written that he would not let his wife go back to the Land of Soviets which they had suffered to much to leave. The memory was awful . . . And then they still had to escape from Poland, where bandits roamed at nights killing communists – or preferably Jews. Alf was lame at that time, and Nadka scarcely alive after a miscarriage, but they had to cross two frontiers and then wait six years in Bavaria for an American visa. So there was no way he would allow Nadka back to the USSR now. 'Come and visit us if you can,' he would say. 'We'll receive you as part of the family. You'll like it here, for where better is there to live than here, where people don't disturb each other or fear the NKVD . . .'

And so Cholyshev sat about on the balcony by day, and by night he listened to all the knocks and rustles and voices on the stairs, and especially to the quiet monologues confided to the portable telephone. It seemed as if the flat was occupied not by one family but by three individuals, each regarding the presence of the others as almost an encroachment on his own freedom. They all lived separately, slept separately, ate separately, and even prayed in different rooms. In Grisha's hung an unrestored, evidently seventeenth-century icon with two little shrines, while Masha had a crude modern one.

If Svetlana was not at home, Masha would take the telephone into their little bedroom, but she spoke very guardedly, peppering her side of the conversation with interjections and scraps of songs, aphorisms and jokes which were unfamiliar to the old man. Only when speaking about Nadya did she talk plainly. The possible arrival of her sister-in-law irritated her. Instead of throwing away money on air tickets she could send her niece something for her wardrobe: the poor girl had nothing to wear.

Nothing to wear? thought the old man angrily. She runs about in Zhenya's skirts and jumpers.

Grisha would take the telephone into his room after midnight, and usually rang Mark's wife. Cholyshev no longer thought anything of this. After all, a man has to unburden his heart to someone if his wife has turned away from him.

In the morning Grisha got up first, snorted a bit in the bathroom, then tiptoed through Cholyshev's room to wake Svetlana. Squabbling, they would hiss at each other: 'Don't bawl, you'll wake everybody up . . .'

But the old man would have woken up long before that, and Masha, having either come home drunk or stunned herself with sleeping pills, did not get up before middday.

Once he had given his daughter breakfast and seen her off, Grisha gave no signs of life until three o'clock. Sometimes, it is true, losing his temper with Masha for what he considered excessive spending, Tokarev would set about doing the housework, running to the shops, and madly rattling saucepans in the kitchen. This would last a day or two, until the money ran out, and the food was worse than ever.

The food here gave the old man stomach pains, and he spent ages in the toilet.

'Stuck in there again!' Masha would mutter outside the door, and Cholyshev would recall his free life with Zhenya, when there was always a bowl of fruit in the living-room, which he could eat whenever he pleased. The Tokarevs bought only apples and oranges occasionally for Svetlana.

Père Goriot! – Cholyshev mocked at himself. One day you'll wake up and there will be nothing to clean your teeth with.

While he was in hospital, Masha had received his pension, and now too he gave her everything – down to the last kopeck. That was why he never went outside: his pockets were empty. Masha for her part did not offer her father any money. So all he had was his little balcony, and his Spidola radio which had started working again. Its imagined disability proved to have been most opportune. Otherwise it would not have escaped the lot of Zhenya's bureau and the kitchen furniture, which Masha gave to the former neighbours for a pittance. They had recently stopped jamming Western stations, and Pashet sat for hours rocking the muffled-up wireless on his knees.

He sometimes wondered whether he should telephone Filipp . . . But he couldn't invite him here – nor go to his place. And would he be in, anyway? If he wasn't dead, he would have gone back to work, and have no time for Pashet. No, it wouldn't be good to let Filipp see him as such an old dodderer. He would laugh.

Cholyshev often remembered one of his old hospital mate's stories: 'Old age, Pashka, senility – you can't fight it. My wife's aunt lives with us. Do you know what she gets up to on pension day? The minute she gets her hands on those forty sacred roubles she orders a taxi. She has to buy a cake, you see, and visit a friend. "Now take me to Vozdvizhenka Street," she says to the taxi-driver. His eyes pop out of his head. He probably wasn't even born when Vozdvizhenka became Kalinin Street. How they solve the problem, I don't know, but no sooner does the driver deliver her to the required address, than the lady remembers that her bosom pal no longer lives there. She moved long ago to the Vagankov Cemetery! Then, so that the cake should not go to waste, the lady orders the driver to take her to Myasnitskaya Street. They go through the same comedy, and finally on Kirov Street she remembers that her Myasnitskaya friend is also resting somewhere you can't reach by taxi. To cut a long story short, after the fourth or fifth attempt the old dear is hysterical, and returns "*nach Hause*" with the squashed cake pressed against her chest. The twelfth of every month is D-day in our house. I've started telling my wife: "Take her pension from her. She'll croak one of these days in a taxi!" Some hope! The old lady would beat you off with her stick . . .'

Well, I don't think I'm senile, but I've no pension either . . . Cholyshev made a wry face. It was after one o'clock in the morning. Through the wall, his son-in-law was pledging his love to Mark's wife. It seemed the *Yeshibotnik* was to be let out of hospital next day, and in a week they would be in Vienna.

'Lena, I have the gift of prophecy! We will meet . . . We can't part for ever. You'll see: we shall be together, and very soon . . .' Tokarev was in full flood.

Lord, does he have to lie when he's saying goodbye? thought Cholyshev, and heaved a sigh.

But one pension-day morning Masha said to her father: 'Dad, it's not good for you in the living-room. Move into the separate bedroom. Grishka's finished his novel.'

His love story, you mean – thought Pashet. But aloud he muttered that he preferred the living-room, with its balcony.

'But the living-room is for Svetka. You can sit there all you like while she's at school.'

So they're moving in together again, Cholyshev guessed, and stood his ground: 'I think it would be more convenient for *you* in the separate room.'

'It would suit us best *this* way. Don't argue.'

'Well, you could put Svetlana in the separate room. She wanted . . .'

'She wants a lot of things! She wants a sheepskin coat too. How can I get her a sheepskin coat?!' said Masha peevishly, but Cholyshev knew that she would get her daughter a sheepskin coat somehow. Masha was as helpless before Svetlana as old Cholyshev was before Masha.

'Grishka, take your things through,' cried Masha, and Tokarev shamefacedly carried his books, notebooks, icon, sheets and torn trousers through to the little chamber off the living-room.

'There, you see, it's better here. You've even got your own day-bed back.' Masha made a face, but Cholyshev did not see it. He felt uncomfortable, and said with a sigh: 'You didn't do a very good swap, did you?'

'It was a rotten swap, Dad. Terrible. You can't even imagine how bad it was. It's rotten. Everything's rotten. *I'm* rotten . . .' Suddenly Masha buried her face in her father's jacket and cried. How he had dreamed of that, and here it was . . . But now the old man was frightened. 'Oh, Dad, it's all gone wrong . . . With you too . . . We shouldn't have moved in together. Am I such a

skinflint? It's just a hellish life. Whatever I do it turns out wrong
. . . And yet I'm not such a freak, I'm not stupid . . . They used to
say I was capable – you'll conquer the world, they said. You'll have
men at your beck and call. In fact, I've drudged for them like a
slave. How come I'm such a failure? Other women are stupider and
uglier – and they get pampered. What's wrong with me?'

You're not feminine enough, her father sighed to himself
bitterly. You always wanted to have things your own way, you
even had to be kind to others in your own way . . .

'I always had to jump at things,' Masha went on, as though
overhearing her father's thoughts. 'I didn't know how to wait and
be patient. What a stupid way to behave! My whole life slipped by
in a rush: I'd always start one thing before I'd finished another,
and never did anything properly. But look at how much I had to
cope with! Everyone assumed I was strong, I could stand it. Look
at Grishka – he's an angel, but it's me who drags him along. He's
turned grey already, but psychologically he's just a boy. He's a
romantic. He lives in a dream world . . . doesn't want to know
about ordinary life. He's never even learned how to earn money
. . . So I tire myself out for everybody, and please nobody. Mum
never saw my help, and Viktor is neglected, even if he is married.'

Where does Viktor come into it? her father wondered. What's he
got to complain about? He steals meat from the cold stores, and
Bronka left him her dacha . . .

'Viktor's neglected,' Masha wept, 'and so are you, Dad . . .
There wasn't enough of me for you all. I dried up . . .'

'What are you saying, lass? You've still got –'

'No, Dad. I'm rotten, there's too much rottenness in me!' Masha
sobbed, and her father, comforting her, felt a semblance of
happiness, inasmuch as this is possible for an old widower
deprived of his home and customary style of life.

But that was not the only miracle. The postwoman brought his
pension, and Cholyshev laid it on top of Zhenya's once shining
refrigerator. But within minutes Masha burst into the closet and
gave him back all twelve ten-rouble notes.

Pashet was glad that his daughter had come into money. But now he felt ashamed that out of fear of Masha he had not given the postwoman her customary rouble. However, he decided not to let such a good morning be overshadowed. He pulled on his galoshes, which he had bought himself, and which Zhenya had threatened to throw out. It was usually she who had bought his footwear. His last pair of Finnish boots, lined with white fur, were particularly good. But today Grisha had gone out wearing them.

Much more lightly dressed than for the balcony, Cholyshev carefully went down the stairs, and made his way slowly along the unfamiliar street, testing the snow with great concentration lest he slip.

Today Cholyshev was filled with curiosity about the neighbourhood, this wasteland which bore about as much resemblance to Timbuktu as it did to Moscow. But for some reason it had been merged into the capital and covered with five-, nine- and twelve-storey buildings, some speckled, some chequered, some just greyish-white. Somewhere around there ought to be a laundry, named 'Seagull' in Chekhovian style, where Pashet was taking his shirts, so as not to burden Masha. Then he would go to the barber's and the grocery shop. That would suffice for the first time. Still, what was taking place was a great revival – almost a resurrection from the half-dead.

But in the glass hall of the laundry he had to queue for an hour and a half in the stuffy heat, and in the end the girl assistant shouted insolently that the identification marks on the collars were illegible (Masha took her anger out on them when she washed!) and flung four of the five shirts back at him. At the barber's shop the sweaty, big-breasted assistant, stinking of garlic and more besides, made a face to her girlfriends, as if to say: 'This customer is past it: all he'll need is a shave and trim . . .'

True enough, my mug is prehistoric, thought the old man, looking at the mirror with contempt. It's as if in my dotage I'd remembered to shave but forgotten to die . . .

Exhausted by the long contemplation of his exterior, Pashet

crept out once more into the slippery avenue, which it had not even occurred to the good-for-nothing yard-keepers to sand. He was terrified of breaking his leg, and reached the shop only by some miracle.

In the sausage section there was a queue, in the confectionery section likewise, and in the partitioned-off wine section people were jostling and swearing, and thrusting greedy shaking hands with notes and coins past the other customers' heads . . .

And so out again into the slippery street, now with the added fear of breaking bottles and crushing a cake. Cholyshev did not have a sweet tooth, and bought the cake merely as a challenge to Filipp's story about the old lady: as if to say, we may be old, but we're a long way from our dotage yet . . .

But for a long time he was unable to find his block of flats. As though to spite him, all the blocks on his street were absolutely alike. He eventually found the right one and climbed to the fourth floor, stopping on every half-landing. He was more worn out than after years of war.

'You've been gallivanting,' Masha reproached him affection-ately, but still did not look at him. She's not really thinking about me either, Pashet guessed.

Tokarev arrived home in his father-in-law's new boots. He was also acting strangely today, but whether his excitement was due to success or failure was impossible to tell.

'Did you find out?' asked Masha. Tokarev shrugged his shoulders indeterminately.

'Right, Dad. Go and rest now. We're going to have lunch in the living-room today.'

Pashet stretched out in his broad day-bed. His heart was beating faster even than in the autumn when Masha had rushed over with the telegram.

'It probably was a heart attack, though . . . The medicos missed it . . . I had it standing up . . .' Cholyshev whispered, mimicking the lively Filipp Semyonovich's intonation.

'Have courage!' replied his hospital neighbour, appearing out of the blue. 'It won't be any worse . . . You've lost the woman you love – your wife. So spit on everything. Go out on to your balcony and spit – up or down, whatever you like, because God doesn't exist in any case. Would He have orphaned you, a decrepit, helpless old man, and then shoved you into this cage of a room?!'

'But they put me into the best room.'

'They'll cheat you. Rub your eyes, and keep your ears pricked up, because people like you always get outwitted . . .'

. . . Filipp must have died, Cholyshev suddenly decided. Covered in sweat, he felt suffocated in the tiny room, where even his own bed seemed foreign. Although it was March the central heating was on full blast. His heart was thumping – racing and faltering in turns like a badly tuned engine. He was scared to move . . . And his voice had vanished: he had no strength to shout for the window to be opened, and his whisper would not be heard during the day, even if the wall was rotten.

Nevertheless he recovered, and an hour later, when the four of them sat down at a fairly clean tablecloth, he drank two glasses of vodka. The vodka stimulated him, the pain subsided in his chest, and he felt delighted that they were all gathered together at last; the *borshch* wasn't marvellous but it was hot and served with sour cream, and his daughter had served him first – just as in that long-forgotten life his mother had served his father and Leokadia Klim. It was cool in the room. Despite Svetlana's cold, the balcony door was ajar.

But suddenly Masha's face aged and blackened, and she cried out in anguish: 'Dad, we're at rock bottom . . .'

She was no longer hiding her eyes from him, and they had a persecuted look about them.

'Masha, wait – why launch into it like that?' Tokarev tried to calm her.

'Oh, what does it matter how we start? In short, Dad, We've no money, and can't borrow any.'

'But just today you gave me back . . .'

'God! What's your pension got to do with it? What do we need it for? As if money means anything to us! We'd gladly starve, if only there was something worth starving for. But we're up to our necks in shit. I can't get a job. They've been chucking out Grishka's articles for over two years, and if he so much as showed his prose to anyone he'd end up in jail. And Svetka will never get into college. In other words, we've got to get out of here. Let's go, Dad!'

'What-at?!' Cholyshev turned purple.

'We must leave, Dad. We can't live here any more. Our illusions are dead. Grishka and I used to think we could get by somehow, living quietly, and honestly. There was a time like that – during Khrushchev's fragile thaw and for a year or so after it. Grisha was printed. He managed to wrap up a few germs of progressive thought in Marxist quotations like glass in straw. He hated all this packaging, but put up with it. Like a fool he thought he was working for the good of democracy . . . But in actual fact they were duping him. And in the long run, G. Tokarev was serving a demonic power, albeit with certain reservations. But now a critic can't work with reservations. And it's a good thing he can't! He doesn't need to soil his hands. Do you remember how you lost your temper, Dad, because I attacked the Church in *Science and Religion*? You were right to lose your temper. What did I understand then? But now you could hang, draw and quarter me and I wouldn't write such a thing. So what if they won't employ me – too bad! I won't have to sell myself any more. Because to live here and not sell yourself is impossible! We've already tried everything. We worried, and suffered, always hoping we would achieve something – that we would push back the limits of legality. It would become easier to live, freer to breathe. Would it hell!! All we were doing was collaborating with the authorities; we were unprincipled, like everyone else . . . But now everything has clarified itself: the majority are unashamedly on the make – they work for the clothes they can buy, trips abroad, and so on, while the minority – no, not even the minority, but a few dozen heroes – have become dissidents . . . And so we must leave. They're letting people out now, thank God. Are we going to miss the chance? We can leave, and purify ourselves, wash ourselves clean . . . Since we can't join the dissidents, we must leave. If I was alone I might have become a dissident, but what kind of fighters are *they*?!' Masha looked with fear at her daughter and husband. 'They're not fit for Lefortovo.* Let's go, Dad . . . It can't be helped – you and I have built this prison, but we don't necessarily have to hang around till we're put in it!'

'What prison?' shouted the old man. 'Oh, that poem . . . I've come to terms with that. For the information of those present,' he looked sullenly at his son-in-law, 'I have never built prisons. And I haven't had anything to do with coal mines for seventeen years.'

'But do they pay you a pension?' asked Masha, becoming embittered. 'What for, I wonder? I'll tell you what for – for building, that's what for! So you've earned your pension well – all one hundred and twenty crisp roubles of it!'

'But . . .' Cholyshev immediately checked himself, realizing that Masha was just waiting for him to object: 'So how come you accepted *that* pension from me?' and then she would pounce on him for 'reproaching' her, kick up a row, and by then it would be too late to dissuade her.

'Calm down, girl. You're upset. We'll speak later . . .' he muttered. He could not bring himself to say anything more worthwhile. But in his thoughts he was not so cowed by his daughter and dared to defend himself: Who says you've got to be either a dissident or an émigré? Either a servant or a fighter? Somewhere between the eithers and the ors you've got at least two hundred and fifty Soviet citizens. They're not fighters, but they're not toadies either. They're just ordinary folk. They live, and adapt themselves as best they can. What categorical imperatives are these? If one must wash oneself clean, then why abroad at all costs? You used to be active here: try and cleanse yourself here . . . And

* A KGB prison in Moscow, used for pre-trial interrogation of dissidents. [Tr.]

Svetlana with her marks wouldn't get to a college anywhere. As for Grishka . . .

But without completing his thoughts about Grishka, Cholyshev blew up: 'I don't understand what writers have to complain about. Sit and write! Nobody's hurrying you.'

'But they don't publish it, Pashet . . . They don't publish anything.' Tokarev blushed.

'And how do the others manage? Look at what's his name . . . how much he has published. And he doesn't particularly try to please the authorities, does he? He just writes about all sorts of little details of life – and gets it just about right.'

'How come you all produce the same argument?!' said Masha angrily. 'You've latched on to this degenerate and bring him up all the time. OK, he gets published – for the time being. But he only spreads nostalgia. He doesn't write anything important: he skirts round all the sharp corners. But how long will he manage to keep his hands clean? He's smart, and careful. Look after number one. Has he ever defended anybody, even once? Not likely! The moment he hears that some friend or comrade is about to be chucked out of the Writers' Union he makes himself scarce. Anybody else would go broke with all those air fares. But mark my words, that brave spirit will pay for it soon. They'll soon cover him, or he'll cover himself, in so much shit that it will be a real pleasure to look at him. No, no one will remain untarnished here.'

'All right, I admit you are better informed about purely literary matters. Let's suppose, then, that it's hard, or even impossible, to get into print here without debasing oneself. But it's still permitted to live, so far. It's not prohibited to converse with one another. Visiting friends and having guests round isn't forbidden. We couldn't even do that. For forty years I was scared to open my mouth. There wasn't a soul I could speak to – except maybe your granddad, Masha . . .'

'You're a special case, Pashet . . .' Grisha smiled, avoiding any mention of Doctor Tokar to be on the safe side.

'It wasn't just me. Everybody was scared.'

'They'll soon be scared again,' Masha predicted, also ignoring the call to remember her murdered grandfather. 'And what's the argument? Since we can get out, we must get out!'

'But everybody can't go, you know! And what's the sense of leaving? The French have a saying: To leave is to die a little. Zhenya left . . .'

'We're not French, we're Jews!' Masha shouted.

Oho! – thought Cholyshev, surprise breaking through his sadness. That's new! I haven't heard that from her before. Does she mean her Polish grandmother? So she would sacrifice anyone for the sake of getting out . . .?

'Don't be stupid, kids,' he said. 'You'll take this game too far if you don't watch out. It's as dangerous as pretending to be mad. These games invariably end up causing pain. Understand, your leaving won't help anything. All your troubles, ailments, quarrels – you won't leave them at the customs: you'll take them with you. And who will you share them with abroad? And what do you think you'll do there, anyway? You belong here. Everything you have is here. Even the whole of your stupid life was rooted here. I admit I often didn't like it, but in the end I came to terms with it. When it comes down to it, there is something in all this depravity and drunken talk . . . Something is growing up out of all the – what at first sight looks like a disgraceful mess. After a long period of dumbness, people are learning – one way or another – to communicate. So the spiritual climate is changing here.' Cholyshev spoke the last words with a funny accent, because high style was not his element. 'You see, Masha, your father has understood you after all. Not at first, it's true, not till he was almost at death's door, but he did understand you. Who will understand you abroad? They don't even know your language. They'll look at you and say you're ne'er-do-wells, hooligans, drunkards . . . and have nothing to do with you . . . Besides, they're up to their necks in their own troubles over there. So just you keep your imperatives, Masha. Even Adenauer wasn't so categorical. Do you remember, before they built the wall, when millions of Germans were escaping by the underground, the old chancellor asked the East German doctors not to leave the Soviet zone. He understood that you couldn't leave people without medical aid. Can you leave them without any aid at all? There is a whole mass of people thronging around you. Perhaps you can achieve something here. And even if you don't, something will still change in the air from your efforts. Forgive your old man for the high-flown words, but stop acting like fools. I mean, emigrating is nothing short of capitulation – an admission that your life in your own country was all in vain. And it's self-deception into the bargain, and also a purely selfish undertaking. Others can't leave, after all. You can't take Ryazan, Kazan, Altai, Kaluga and the rest of the population with you. They can't all move out of Russia. And your departure won't change anything in this country. The women will carry on giving birth, and toiling with their disobedient children, and wearing themselves out with work and housework, and swapping rumours in the queues, and brawling with their drunken husbands. And the men will booze, and curse Soviet power, and have childish dreams that can never come true – and they'll never leave, either. I certainly don't believe that Russia should be opening the eyes of the sinful West. But whatever else may be, this country has seen a lot, and you won't cross it out by leaving. It won't even notice that you've disappeared . . .'

But Masha did not hear her father, and repeated nervously: 'We must go, Dad. We must. We've got an invitation for the four of us. Show him,' she ordered her husband.

'Here, Pashet . . . Can you make it out without your glasses?' Grisha asked diffidently. He felt uncomfortable because they had launched straight into the discussion. They ought to have broken Pashet in gradually. He was an old man, after all.

Cholyshev did not feel like getting up for his spectacle-case. Holding the foreign forms at arm's length, he learned with amazement that a stranger by the name of Rebekka Blum was sincerely concerned about his fate: 'I hereby earnestly request the appropriate competent Soviet authorities to grant my relations permission to leave in order to take up permanent residence with me in Israel.

'After many years of separation and all that we have endured, we share a great desire to reunite our families and to live inseparably in the future.

'My family and I are materially well provided for and have all the means necessary to look after my relatives from the day they arrive.'

'Impressive,' Cholyshev mumbled. He was touched. And no wonder! Here was a strange woman, posing as his relative, willing to take care of him, an old man. He had never once written to his own relations – Klim and Leokadia – and in Europe was afraid of bumping into them . . . Yet this Rebekka was inviting him and offering help.

'Seems to be a good woman,' he said. 'Would you really impose on her like that?'

'Pashet, it's just a model . . . You see, it's even printed . . .' His son-in-law blushed.

'I thought it was for real . . .'

Now the old man was ashamed that for an instant he had believed somebody needed him.

'Let's go, Dad! What have we got to lose?' Masha smiled through tears. 'We'll have a look at how people live. We've never seen anything . . .'

How did she manage to get drunk so quickly? The fool . . . He wished he could make her see sense. Running away . . . and to Israel! When they got there Grisha would leave her for that Lena . . .

'Listen, lass, what's Israel got to offer you?' he grumbled, feeling a burning sensation inside his chest.

'Grandad! Do you want to split them up?' exclaimed Svetlana, pricking up her ears.

'But we're not going to Israel, Dad! Don't you get it? We're going to Nadka's . . . Just let her try not to help us!'

'It gets worse and worse . . . Are you seriously thinking of

173

dragging me to her?! I wouldn't dream of it . . . It's a waste of good paper.' Cholyshev jabbed a finger at the glossy forms. 'Without me they won't let you out, and I'm not going. You were wrong to expose yourself: all this *goes down on your files!*' He pushed aside the forms. 'Why are you so ill-starred?' He looked sorrowfully at his daughter. 'You're always in such a hurry. And now you've landed yourself in fresh trouble. Don't you see – this is like a self-denunciation!'

'We've got another one . . .' said Grisha, growing gloomier. And Cholyshev was informed that Israeli citizen Benjamin Schneider regarded as his relatives only Grigory and Svetlana Tokarev, plus Maria Cholyshev.

'In that case good luck to you . . .' Pashet sighed, and said not another word all evening. The news overwhelmed the old man, and swamped every vessel in his head, so that he became impervious to everything.

The railwayman arrived. But Pashet did not notice him and did not hear his daughter's pipe-dreams about how they could wangle it so that Viktor would be registered at this address.

'Nothing will come of it,' Grisha gloated. 'We must be beyond suspicion. Otherwise they'll find fault with us for fiddling the residence regulations.'

'But he is my brother . . .'

'Makes no difference.'

'But I told you to find out about it!' Masha shouted in annoyance.

'I only found out about these . . .' Tokarev cautiously moved both invitations from the table on to the windowsill, further from his brother-in-law.

'Aren't you going?' the Viking asked the old man, as usual omitting his name.

'Gh-t-t . . .' Cholyshev growled, coming to for a moment and then drifting away again.

'He's shouting me down again, Masha. Is that a forbidden question?'

'Maybe we'll both go?' Masha embraced her brother. 'It's terrible to leave you.'

'Why?! I'll be all right. I don't need much – I don't have any leadership ambitions,' Viktor grinned, forgetting that he had not even finished his ten-year schooling. 'If I get your shack, that'll do me. There's this bloke in our town, started out a country type, and now I meet him and he's some kind of foreign-relations boss of something or other. They offered him a five-room apartment, he says, and he turned it down. Wanted two bathrooms and two bogs. "I can't use the same conveniences as the servant," he says. I'm not so fussy, though.'

'You won't get a bloody thing,' snarled Tokarev.

'Oh, to hell with the lot of you,' shouted Masha and burst into tears. 'Go away, Viktor. I'll think of something. I'll manage. Go on. My head is splitting . . .'

It would have been obvious to the blind that Masha was at breaking point, but her father's strength was also gone.

'Coma . . . I'm becoming weightless . . .' he whispered, and scarcely made it to his bed.

'Dissidence begins with the letter-box,' Tokarev hurriedly scribbled in his disintegrating ledger. 'I receive no Writers' Club calendars, no invitations to concerts or book-lovers' gatherings, nothing. I used to throw all that bumf straight into the dustbin, but now I miss it somehow. Pashet imagined that everything was "hunky-dory" with me. He doesn't believe that it is not at all easy for me to leave him, old and withered as he is . . . But will they let us out, anyway? We are hanging between heaven and earth.

'What will happen if they turn us down, or stall for even a year? Pashet made up his mind that all we had to do was want to go, and we could . . . He did not even inquire about what happened at the Writers' Union when I went for a character reference for the Visa Office. And yet what they did to me was a real civil execution . . .

'One day, perhaps, I shall write a novel or story about it, but meanwhile – a few words to help the memory.

'. . . Twenty Moscow secretaries fulminated to the best of their abilities. Some shouted that I had become a dissident and there was nothing surprising in that. They had suspected that I would end up that way. When I tried to object that I had not been involved in any extra-literary activities, some other secretaries nodded: "Yes, you're not a dissident, you're an anti-Soviet." It was not without reason that they had not seen my articles for a long time. For that reason, before giving me a character reference they would have to check what I was writing. Perhaps I had passed slanderous material to the West.

'I replied that I was working as a critic, just as before, and that if my articles were not printed, it certainly was not my fault. "No," they retorted, "it is your fault: your articles are rejected precisely because they are anti-Soviet."

'A third group branded me a Zionist because I was forsaking a country which had established a fraternity of peoples for a dubious chauvinist state in which the Arabs were oppressed. (I could not tell them that I am going to America. They would have burst with envy, even though they themselves pop over there twice a year.)

'A fourth set, mainly my former friends with whom I have drunk gallons of vodka, gloomily questioned me about who Benjamin Schneider was. They couldn't seem to remember my mentioning such a relative of mine before. They knew my children from my first marriages, and my old father-in-law, too. But the children and Masha's father were staying in Moscow. So what kind of reunification of families was this?! More like a dismembering! (And I could not tell them that I was going to my blood sister.)

'A fifth group jeered brazenly: "Let him get out of here. It will be no loss. The air will improve immediately if we send *that lot* packing . . ." (They did not even try to conceal that they meant the Jews!)

'Yet another group – the Jewish secretaries – were especially indignant. How could he dare to leave his motherland! His motherland which fed, clothed and reared him! "I understand," said one, "that Tokarev's childhood was not easy. His father was the victim of unfounded repression. But then, the Party has decisively condemned Stalin's cult, and Tokarev's father was posthumously pardoned. Besides, Tokarev himself has never suffered any discrimination. On the contrary. Until only recently almost every number of our best magazine contained either an article or a review of his. He was published, in my view, perhaps even too readily."

'Oh yes? I thought. You used to fall at my feet begging me to write just one little page about you.

' "I don't know if Tokarev is anti-Soviet," this Jew concluded, "but he is manifestly a traitor."

'The next Jew said that I was not persistent enough and too quick to take offence. Was it so awful if I wasn't published?! I ought to put up a fight. If one editor rejected an article, I should take it elsewhere. He had also had a novel turned down by three magazines – *Moscow*, *Young Guard* and *Our Contemporary*. But he had not thrown in the towel. He had kept fighting. And now another eminent magazine (out of superstition he would not say which) had signed a contract with him, and the "Soviet Writer" publishing house had included the novel in its publishing plan. Whereas Tokarev had lost his head and taken offence – and ended up a dissident and a traitor. (I suspect that this secretary considered himself an exceptionally brave and worthy person. And so he was! He clearly implied that certain magazines would not publish Jews. And so what if he took a swipe at me – they were all kicking me. Moreover – I was leaving the USSR, while he had to live here and be published.)

'In short, all twenty men and women spoke, some of them twice. Then they raised their hands together, and the first secretary announced to me that I was unanimously expelled from the Union of Soviet Writers. My character reference, he said, would be sent to the Visa Office, but he did not hint at what they would write in it. (And those in the know say that the reference is crucial to the decision whether to let one out or not. But one can never guess one's fate . . .)

'Thus I became a "renegade", and, worse still, a parasite. Every day I expect a notice from the police: find a job, Citizen Tokarev, or we shall bring you to trial under Article . . . For that reason I suppose the empty letter-box is actually a joy. Although the district police officer could come in person, if he was ordered to creep up to the fourth floor . . .'

Whatever the weather, old Cholyshev was perched on the balcony, but he did not listen to the radio any more: he had enough to think about without it.

What's it to me, this place? – He was looking at the mountain of boxes which had blackened over the winter . . . Is this Russia? There is snow, certainly . . . but there's not much left, and no more will fall until November. Snow – that's Russia, all right. Though half of my life I hardly ever saw any: what kind of snow do you get in the Ukraine? Just this sort of stuff, springlike . . .

To the right and to the left of the boxes, old five-storey 'Khrushchoby'* clung to the tall concrete blocks like waifs.

Maybe you should leave, after all? Cholyshev tormented himself. No, I don't want to. Let Grishka escape. He's been run off his feet, the poor lad . . . He's wavered from hope to hopelessness, then back to hope after the Twentieth Congress, and now all he sees ahead is a void. But why should I move away? I was never greatly taken by this place anyway, so I don't feel let down by it. Even before the Revolution I didn't particularly like it, and afterwards all the more so. When Klim went off to fight with Denikin's White Army I could see where it was all leading to and didn't expect any universal happiness to come of it. I didn't expect it later either – neither when Trotsky was ranting in the former merchants' hall, nor when I myself was firing pistol shots into the air on Victory Day. But Masha and Grisha were always hoping for something. They fell passionately in love with Russia, and now, just as passionately, they curse it and want to make a clean break

* A pun on the Russian for 'slums' (*trushchoby*) and Khrushchev, during whose rule these houses were built.

with it. They are too impatient – they want a happy life immediately, or at least the hope of one in the near future. But how can you promise them anything when there is nothing bright on the horizon? The kids are too used to thaws. But to be honest, I have never really noticed any warmth. It feels like it has been winter all my life. One has always had to muffle oneself up, never throwing open one's coat, and above all not bustling about. There is no need to hurry anywhere in winter: winter is a time of self-knowledge. But the kids rushed around and never thought anything through properly. As a result they had nothing but miscalculations and failures. That's why they attacked me with their 'Stonemason, stonemason...' How did it go on? I remember I went to the trouble of going to the library, copying it out and learning it . . . 'Stonemason, one day perhaps he'll remember / Those who carried the bricks.' It was the stonemason's son who would remember them, when he ended up in that prison. But the father, that is, the stonemason himself, answered: 'Hey, watch out, get away from the scaffold! / We know what we're doing, so keep quiet!'

And quite right, too. Keep quiet. Instead of calling people names . . . The old man felt angry, forgetting that it was Zhenya who had christened him a stonemason, not his daughter and son-in-law.

A stonemason . . . But what could I do? Since I didn't leave with Klim, all that remained was to build – literally and figuratively. And if I am a mason, then why should I leave? I built here, and it's here that I'll receive my stone and lie under it. There is no reason for me to latch on to some other power. I didn't build in any other country, I have no share in its wealth, and who wants to live by begging in a foreign country? What's the point of looking for new troubles when I'm up to my neck in old ones? The kids feel awkward about leaving me . . . Never mind, they'll get by. As if it would be easier to take me with them! I'll drag myself along to the almshouse or the crematorium somehow . . .

So the old man sat, oblivious to the drip of thawing snow, and although they no longer closed the balcony door he was now totally cut off from all the family news, disputes, reconciliations and fresh scandals, which alternated in the Tokarev household with depressing regularity.

'Has he gone deaf?' Masha wondered aloud.

'He's gone soft in the head . . .' Svetlana tapped her temple.

'Do you know what? Let's marry him off!' Grisha suggested.

'Daddy, you silly goat!' Svetlana giggled, but Masha at once started going through the possible brides.

'But we must be tactful,' said Tokarev. 'After Zheka it won't be easy . . .'

'Oh go to hell with your Zheka. What a toff she was!' Masha shouted, but immediately took fright that her father might hear. 'I'm sorry, Grishka . . . It's my nerves. Stop me if I go too far.'

'Dad, you can't be left on your own,' she said one evening, going into her father's tiny bedroom. He was in bed. Masha sat down beside him, and he stroked her shock of grey hair, which she had not dyed for a long time.

'I'm perfectly all right, lass. I don't need anybody.'

'In that case, come with us. We can try a different solution. If you don't want to be dependent on Nadka I'll try and get you a pension. In America everyone over a certain age gets one – and you fought the Nazis into the bargain. The European communities appreciate that.'

'Let's go, Pashet,' said his son-in-law. He had come in unnoticed. Thin, still handsome, and shy like a boy, his head touched the top of the door-frame.

'No . . .'

'But why not?'

'It's simpler to die here.'

'But you'll outlive the lot of us!' Tokarev smiled. 'But even if . . . I mean . . . you would be with Zheka . . .'

'Go away.' The old man turned round, and Masha waited a

moment and then followed her husband out of the room.

What the writers' secretariat wrote to the Visa Office remained a secret, but the Tokarevs received permission to emigrate. They were given only ten days to get ready, however, and those days sped past in haste and confusion. The summer days merged with the short nights, and the front door was never closed, as though there were a dead person in the flat. The living-room was chock-a-block with all kinds of suitcases – new synthetic-leather ones, bought on credit, and old rickety ones (so-called 'Jewish' ones, as they are strong enough to withstand only a one-way journey), as well as packing cases, baskets, cardboard boxes, bundles, and sundry goods and chattels that were not yet packed away.

'What are you taking so much stuff for?'

'It's ludicrous!'

'Don't get carried away, for goodness' sake!'

'Only the very very minimum!'

There was no shortage of advice from friends.

'It's true, Masha, we're overdoing it. Nadka will give us everything we need,' Tokarev reasoned.

'She won't give us a damn!' Masha snapped back.

It was difficult to get through to the balcony, and they were also packing in Cholyshev's room. So he ensconced himself in a corner and answered all questions with an inaudible mutter. An outsider would have thought he had gone quite dotty.

'Do you know, I understand why he wouldn't agree to come,' Masha whispered to her husband. 'He's safeguarding his memories.'

'Hardly . . . You can remember abroad, too.'

'But he has never been abroad. He belongs here entirely. He only has memories of here. All his thoughts, fears, even his ravings – none of them are fit for export.'

'You could say he was never really here, either . . . He always stood on the sidelines, never got involved in anything. And now he doesn't even go outside. In my opinion, it's all much simpler: deep down, you and I hope to come back, but he can never expect to do that. For him, "there will never be another woman".' Tokarev frowned, remembering the night of his departure from Siberia, Nadya's guitar, and Zheka – still quite young in those days, even younger than Lena.

'No, no, that's not it,' Masha insisted. 'Dad has lived seventy – or how many is it – years here, and witnessed everything that happened here. He lived here as an "unfree" mason, as Zhenya put it. He hid himself away here. But he did it all *here*! And now he is turning it all over in his mind – both what he has lived through, and what is happening now. What is there for him to occupy himself with in America? Nobody will understand him there, and – what's far more important to him – he won't understand anybody or anything. The last things he has – his memory and his pangs of conscience – will be taken away. And what will he get in return? Clothes? More comfortable living conditions? Impressions of a new country? He's indifferent to all that. No, he has never been in America and there is nothing for him to do there.'

'But we haven't been there either.'

'That's exactly the trouble. We've never been there, so we never will be. I'm scared that this is all for nothing, Grisha. All for nothing.' Masha glanced at her husband, and instead of bursting into tears, turned away coldly.

'We are leaving at others' expense,' Grisha hastily scribbled down, not in his ledger now, but just on a piece of paper he happened to come across. 'Lena fought with the *druzhinniki** when they dragged her out of the Central Telegraph Office. Jewish friends went on hunger strikes, argued their way into the reception offices of the Supreme Soviet, the Ministry of Internal Affairs, and the Central Committee, and finally breached their resistance. Thanks to them I am leaving Russia – and not even for Israel. So it turns out, I'm a parasite, no more, no less. And yet I am a Russian writer, a man of conscience. I tried to integrate myself with Russia,

* Civilian 'volunteers', marked by red arm-bands, who help the police to maintain law and order in the streets.

I grieved over it, but suddenly realized it did not need me – and opted for America. Ridiculous and stupid . . . What do I know about that country? Who needs me over there, apart from Nadka? And even she . . .

'Masha is right: we have lived here, and there is nothing of us over there. When you are coming on for fifty you can't start a new life. Pashet is also right: emigration smacks of capitulation. All my life, my sufferings, my hopes – are crossed out at a stroke.

'Of course, I could try auto-psychotherapy: I could convince myself that I am going to America to fight for a free Russia, that I shall organize a magazine there and drag Russian literature out of the underground into the light of day. But . . . I'm no fighter, or organizer. Life in this country has worn me down and I am not fit for life over there any more.

' "Two feelings are equally close to us," wrote Pushkin. "Love of one's hearth and home, and love of one's forefather's graves." Naturally, I never searched for my father's remains, but I went to find my mother soon after the war. Aunt Susanna helped me. The same converted goods trains in which we had escaped from the Germans were still running. I went straight from the station to the Jewish cemetery, but there was nothing left of it. A factory was being built nearby, and it was not clear who had removed the stone wall and destroyed the tombstones – the Germans, the local population, or the builders' bulldozers.

'I crawled about in the former graveyard for about four hours until I found a few pieces of marble containing the letters "O", "R", "A" and "K". Whether they used to be part of "DORA TOKAR" I do not know. I left the town that same day and have never been back. Today it is about three times as large as it was before the war. As for the marble fragments, they have not survived our frequent removals . . .

'So either Pushkin got it wrong, or I am a monster, because it is not graves or hearth and home that I am sorry to leave behind, but something else, which I cannot even express . . . It is not what I am leaving that grieves me, but what will come to pass here when I am gone. I remember my fellow students who were invalided in the war complaining that their amputated legs ached. But what about the soul? You can't get an artificial replacement for that! Some people bravely pretend that when they leave they will immediately forget this country. But I know in advance that it will not be like that for me. I shall remain here entirely. I shall think only about this country. I shall beg every new arrival from Russia to tell me what it is like there. What are people thinking, doing, writing? With my last cents I shall buy *Pravda*, which I haven't opened for years, or I shall shed tears over some silly little review in the *Literary Gazette*. And I shall yearn for the vodka queues, for those long and muddle-headed Russian dinner-parties, for the drunkards in empty suburban trains, and I shall probably never fully understand why I left . . .'

And so finally the visas were paid for. (Creditors, do not worry! Nadka will return your kindness somehow or other.) The Tokarevs' belongings were packed up and taken to the Customs Office. Svetlana, to her great joy, obtained her school-leaving certificate without any examinations. There remained only the final evening – the farewell party.

There were more people packed into the flat than there had been at the funeral party a year before, and Pashet hoped to lose himself in the crush. But among the Tokarevs' new 'refusenik' friends, who had been kept waiting for several years, and among those who had only recently applied to leave or were considering whether to apply or wait a while, were their old friends. The latter were getting drunk and rowdy. Particularly obstreperous was the bearded fellow who had once promised to lift the sorrow from old Cholyshev's soul. Now, embracing and shaking him, he was shouting about how Pavel Rodionovich was a real Russian man and that was why he was staying put. And those who were running away were rats, although Russia would never sink. And in general, it wasn't Christian to abandon a lonely helpless old man . . .

Pashet was also pestered by the Amazon and Zhenya's other

female friends, all promising support – some quite sincerely, others inspired by the moment or the vodka. Even when he at last beat them off and squeezed through to the kitchen, he was out of luck again. There, clasping his sister in his mighty hands, Viktor the railwayman was howling frenziedly, while his middle-aged, countrified wife hammered on his massive back.

. . . Still, the company finally began to disperse, and by about three in the morning the last guests left. But it was too late to go to bed. Svetlana laid her head down for a while, but Masha and Grisha wandered about the flat aimlessly, too drained even to sweep the floor. Or perhaps they did not want to out of superstition.

'Dad, you're worn out. Don't see us off. Go to bed,' said Masha, sighing. 'I've asked the yard-keeper's wife to clean up in here.'

'She's right, Pashet, it's not worth it. It's hard to get back here from Sheremetyevo,' said Tokarev, and immediately felt embarrassed. It sounded as if he was superstitiously afraid for himself and his family – as though he was thinking: Pashet saw Zhenya off, and look what happened . . .

'All right, I won't see you off,' the old man nodded.

An alarm-clock rang, and Svetlana jumped up. There were embraces, cries, tears and frantic kisses all round . . . But then the door banged and Cholyshev was left alone. He walked through the flat, and not believing in the mythical yard-keeper's wife, started tidying up. Whether he swept up or not, the Tokarevs would not return. There was enough work to keep him busy till evening.

Then, no longer fearing Masha's criticism, he got into the shower and turned it on full, but suddenly he felt ill and barely made it to his day-bed. After resting a while, he decided to change his bed-linen, but the sheets left behind in the wall-cupboard turned out to be full of holes. Cholyshev imagined that he would spend all night tossing and turning on them; in fact he fell asleep at once.

That night the old man dreamed of Klim. He had once again put on his cassock and had become incredibly huge, such as he had appeared to Pasha Cholyshev only in his distant childhood. Klim's beard was not red, however, but quite grey, as though he were the Lord God himself. Where the old man was standing – indoors, or under the open sky – was also unclear. Uncle Klim was not like his old self. Cholyshev did not try particularly hard, however, to find out if this really was his uncle or not.

'I'm in a bad way, Klim,' said the old man. 'You see, I haven't achieved anything . . . I didn't live a good life . . . And I don't think I acted meanly, or slyly, or elbowed anybody aside. I had no desire to boss people around. On the contrary, you might say I scarcely poked my nose out of my burrow. But Zhenya, my wife, was bored and miserable with me, and the kids christened me a stonemason, and then left me, you see. I don't know if things will turn out well for them . . . They're not so young any more.'

'They won't turn out well,' said Klim.

'They didn't for me either . . . What a dog's life it is! Everyone is unhappy. Perhaps I ought to have gone away with you when I was a boy?'

'Hold on – take your time. You're old, but you're in a hurry. And you are whining and looking hurt like a child,' Klim's voice droned. 'Is it such an insult that they called you a stonemason? What were you to do if nothing was being built apart from a prison? Twiddle your thumbs, or what? And it is also a good thing that you didn't leave with me. One should live at home – and die there too. Although, whether at home or away from home, we arrive at the same thing . . .'

'At Death with capital letters?' Cholyshev was overjoyed, because his uncle had dealt with the stonemason business almost too lightly.

'That's right,' Klim laughed. 'TO DEATH AND TO GOD . . .'

'What's that, Klim, have you returned to the Church?'

'I have.'

'But why? Couldn't you speak with God through the window?'

'I could, but I am weak. My life, Pashka, has been like crossing

... not just a field, but a whole ocean.* So for me to be without the Church is like setting out on a stormy sea alone in a flat-bottomed boat. And the Church is like an ocean liner, where everyone has his own cabin.'

'With different classes available?' Cholyshev joked grimly.

'Still as impudent as ever, eh? No letting up in your old age? Well, you're wrong: let's say it's not a ship but a huge raft, where everyone really is on an equal footing.'

'Apart from those at the edges . . .'

'Oh . . . the devil take you! It's always the bravest – those with the greatest faith – who are at the edge of a raft.'

'People like you, you mean, who fell off but didn't drown?'

'Well, if you like . . . I strayed, but I returned none the less. And they were glad to have me back. A prodigal son is dearer than an unrepentant one.'

'So they would take me back too?'

'Do not doubt it. They take everyone out of kindness. But you are no prodigal son, Pashka. You are simply foolish. You wanted to converse with God through the window or from the balcony – and only when you felt the chill in your veins and your bones started seizing up, at that! There are a lot of you cunning old folk who come scurrying back at the very last minute. Tell me honestly: was it just out of laziness that you decided to pray through the window, or would your legs not carry you as far as the church?'

'Partly it was my legs, and partly I felt awkward . . . Running there at the very end – I was ashamed.'

'It's good if you were ashamed. Christ is with you, even through the window. But better still – through one of us. We are sinners ourselves and would understand you, you mischief-maker. We would keep an eye on you on the common raft.'

Leokadia probably told him, thought the old man with fright.

'Don't tremble, Pasha. The Lord is almighty and kind. He has dismissed you and all those like you like schoolchildren for the

* Russian proverb: 'To live your life is not as easy as to cross a field.' [Tr.]

187

summer holidays. He knows you'll come running back on the first day of term.'

'And if not, He'll haul us back?'

'Why should the Lord have to drag you if you are running to Him of your own accord – albeit through the window?'

'And what will happen to me?'

'Nothing will happen. You've had enough. You've suffered a great deal. Now you will rest. Do you understand?'

'I understand . . .' the old man whispered, and woke up.

Klim was gone. The room was empty.

'Must have been dreaming . . . He was teasing me – saying my death would be easy and simple . . .' Cholyshev said angrily. He stared with a feeling of doom through the window at the whitish, almost milky fog, which promised a pain at the back of his head, burning in his chest, and the unalleviated pangs of his still lively conscience.